Contracted To Mr. Collins

The Unusual Proposal

SJ. Turner

Contents

Title Page
Dedication
Prologue — 4
Chapter 1 – The Interview — 10
Chapter 2 — Lunch — 29
Chapter 3 — Skinny Dippin' — 46
Chapter 4 – Max — 73
Chapter 5 – The Car — 89
Chapter 6 – The Messy Maiden — 104
Chapter 7 — Surprise! — 122
Chapter 8 – Jamaica — 145
Chapter 9 – Quality Time — 171
Chapter 10 – A Quick Turn of Events — 189
Chapter 11 – Oh, Hell No! — 210
Contracted to Mr. Collins 2 — 234
About The Author — 236
Praise For Author — 238

To my sister for pushing me forward xoxo

Cozy Reads Publishing

A Cozy Reads Publication, PO Box 58031 Rosslynn RPO, Oshawa, ON L1J 8L6

Copyright © 2021 by SJ. Turner

All rights reserved

This is a work of fiction. Names, characters, places and incidents are the product of the author's imagination. Any resemblance to actual persons, living or dead, business or establishments, events or locales is entirely coincidental.

No part of this publication may be reproduced, distributed, or transmitted in any form or by any means, including photocopying, recording, or other electronic or mechanical methods, without the prior written consent of the publisher, except in the case of brief quotations embodied in critical reviews and specific other non-commercial uses permitted by copyright law. For permission requests, contact the publisher by e-mail, admin@cozyreadspublishing.com "Attention: Permission Request" as the subject line.

Content Notice: Due to explicit adult situations and use of mature language, this book is intended for persons age 18+.

Contracted To Mr. Collins
The Unusual Proposal
By SJ. Turner

ISBN 978-1-7777646-2-3 (E-book)
ISBN 978-1-7777646-1-6 (Pbk)

Fiction — Romance
Fiction — Romance — Erotic Romance
Fiction — ChickLit

Cover Designed by Freelance Arts

Prologue

Aiden isn't at all surprised when he pulls into his driveway and finds Max's hummer parked by the garage. Even though they're almost thirty years old, as identical twins, they still spend most of their spare time together.

He grabs his suit jacket that still bears the latte from this morning's encounter with the young lady he can't seem to get out of his mind and heads inside. The smell of mesquite wafts through the air as he makes his way out to the patio. That's where he finds Max. He's dancing next to the barbeque in a pair of lycra swim shorts with a beer.

Throwing his arm out, Aiden shouts over the music. "Hey! Why's the music so damn loud, and what have I told you about wearing those damn shorts here?"

Max chucks his chin, smiling as he turns around. He places his hand on his rump, rubbing his butt cheek. "Seriously? Do you see the way these make my ass look?" Spinning back, he grabs his noticeable bulge in the front and gives it a shake. "And this" —he winks, his smile broadening— "women love this shit, bro."

Shaking his head, Aiden chuckles. "Right, well, this isn't a strip club, Max." He fans his arm out around the deck. "I don't see any women here at the moment to appreciate it. It's just you and me. So, in the future, wear real shorts."

With a curt nod, Max winks. "Noted." He gulps back his beer, pointing his empty bottle at his brother. "Speaking of which. When are we going to do something about that? I thought you were going to start looking for Mrs. Right."

Tossing his ruined jacket over the back of one of the chairs, Aiden walks behind the bar to retrieve a beer. He twists off the cap and flicks it at Max. "Me? Why haven't *you* found her yet? In case you've missed it, I'm running a corporation. What is it you're doing again?" He holds his hand in the air and shakes his head at Max. "Oh, right. You're too busy playing the playboy while using my name and house to do it. So let me ask again. Why haven't YOU found us a Mrs. Right yet?"

Max squints across the table, eyeing Aiden as he takes his seat. "Wait a minute now. I've given you an amazing catalogue of beautiful women to choose from. Not to mention, had you named as the most eligible bachelor in Victoria." He tips his head with a smirk as he gets up to slather more sauce on the ribs. "Besides, I share the fine prospects that I bring back here with you, don't I?"

The corner of Aiden's mouth lifts as he holds his bottle out toward Max with a nod. "That you do." Drawing his brows together, he tilts his head in question. "Although you seem to forget one thing. I actually want a wife. Not a toy we can share. This hair-brain idea that we should share one – that's all you. I mean, we're not kids anymore, Max, and that's not how marriage works."

"Oh, come on, Aiden. We've been over this a thousand times. You're too busy to keep a wife on your own. She'll get lonely and end up cheating on you. If she's smart enough to have a kid or two, she can take everything you own with her, including half the corporation. The only way to avoid that is to keep her happy while you're busy. That's where I come in. You just get her to sign a contract. You're good with those. Offer her a generous compensation package in exchange for a trial period, let's say six months. We can slowly reveal our plan as she settles into the relationship. It's really that simple." He chucks his chin and points to the stain on Aiden's shirt. "What the hell is that on your shirt anyway?"

Brushing his hand over the stain, the image of the flustered young lady from this morning floods Aiden's mind. She looked so innocent, practically running with her portfolio tucked in her arms while holding that damn latte he wore in her hand. "Well, I guess you could say I had a run-in with a latte this morning."

"You drink lattes now?"

Recalling the look on her face as she watched him wipe off his shirt, he shakes off the image with a smile. "No, but a stunning young lady that was applying for the account executive position seems to like them. She ran into me in the lobby, literally," he says, swiping his hand over the stain. "Hence my run-in with a latte."

"Stunning, huh?" Max flips the ribs he's been slow roasting on the barbeque. "Would you say she's the Mrs. Right type of stunning?"

Aiden slugs back his beer, shrugging with a smirk. "Not likely. She seems like she might be a little sexually naive. Nothing like what you'd be looking for."

Grabbing another beer, Max sits down, resting his forearms on the table. "I'm okay with sexually naive. I love a good challenge. Besides, we can slowly introduce the idea. So why don't you let me sit in on the interview with you?"

"I haven't even said she would get an interview yet, and letting our twin status out of the bag upfront is not a smart idea."

Max nods. "Yeah, you may be right about that," he says, his lips pulling into a sly smile. "But you know damn well she's getting an interview. Shit, I can tell you right now that girl will make it back in just from the look on your face. You'll make sure of it."

"Either way, she's not the one. Not for what you're proposing. If we're even considering sharing a wife, we want someone that's open to trying new things. Someone with a high sex drive and doesn't mind having us both in bed with her on occasion. She has to keep our twin secret and be my wife first and not only for social purposes. It's going to be difficult to find someone who can be a wife and lover, as you're suggesting. Besides, this young lady is merely looking to acquire a job. Seriously, forget I even mentioned this young lady." Aiden waves his hand toward the barbeque. "How long before those ribs are ready? I'm starved."

Pursing his lips, Max nods. "Fine. I won't say another word about her, but if you do call her in for an interview, I'd like to sit in." He lifts the lid on the barbeque and runs his finger over one of the racks of ribs. Stuffing his finger into his mouth, he raises his brows as he licks the sauce off with a smile. "Mmmm, oh, they're done." He shakes his finger at Aiden. "I made this Tennesee Whiskey sauce from scratch. Just for you, little brother."

Wiping his hand over his face, Aiden shakes his head. "I'm sure you did and quit calling me little brother. We're twins."

He glances back at Aiden and waves his hand toward the house. "Yeah yeah, I'm still older. Now, why don't you grab the potato salad that I picked up on my way over? It's in the fridge. Oh, and grab us some plates."

"Oh sure, I just worked all day, but let me get them." Grabbing his suit jacket from the back of the chair beside him, he walks into the house, still cursing under his breath. Aiden hangs his coat on the hook by the front door making a mental note to call the cleaners and heads for the fridge. As he leans in to grab the potato salad, his phone hits the floor, and his personal assistant's name, Natasha, appears on the screen. "Hmm, maybe that's a sign. I guess it couldn't hurt to look over her résumé."

Setting the salad on the counter, he picks up his phone and initiates the call.
'Natasha speaking.'
"Natasha, I brought in a résumé this morning from one of the candidates and left it on your desk. Did you get it?"
'Yes, Sir, I did. A Miss Rebecca D'Angelo. I just added it to the received pile a few minutes ago.'
Aiden runs his hand through his hair smiling at the sound of

her name. "Rebecca. Wonderful. Could you send me a copy? I'd like to look it over."

'Sure. I'll send it over after I'm done eating.'

"Thanks, Natasha. Sorry to bother you during dinner."

'Never a bother, Sir.'

Sliding his phone into the front pocket of his pants, he leans against the counter, running his thumb across his bottom lip. He needs to think of a way to keep Max busy while he checks this girl out. One thing is for certain, he wants to know more about Rebecca D'Angelo. If he can get Max out of town for a few weeks, he can follow her around himself, see what her typical lifestyle is like.

Max leans in the backdoor, his big booming voice interrupting Aiden's thoughts. "Hey! You getting the plates or what?"

He bounces off the counter and spins to grab the plates from the cupboard. "Yes, I'm coming! I was speaking with Natasha."

Setting the plates down on the table by the barbeque, he pats Max on the shoulder. "I'm going to need you to go check out the place in Seattle we talked about last week."

"What? I thought you said you had decided that doing business across the border was too much hassle," Max says, eyeing him suspiciously.

Spooning some potato salad onto his plate, Aiden nods. "Yes, it's a bit of extra paperwork, but Natasha says we're getting a lot of requests from that area. That tells me it could be a worthwhile venture, but we'll need to open a new office out there, and I can't be in two places at once. So, I'm going to need you to go find us a suitable office space and possibly hire a few people to get it up and running."

Looking at Aiden from under his brows, Max leans back in his chair and reaches for his beer. "You want me to not only find an office but hire staff? Are you fucking serious?"

"Yes, I am. You know the type of structure we require, and Natasha will prescreen the candidates for you to hire. I'll have her line up some properties for you to look at, and she can arrange your flight and accommodations tomorrow." Aiden holds his beer up toward Max with a smile. "It's time you did something to earn that handsome paycheck you see each month."

Max shakes his head, his cheeks nearly hitting his eyes as he grins. "Wow! You're really going to trust me with this."

Nodding, Aiden takes a drink of his beer. "Just don't jump on the first place that you see. Be sure to take your time and check out all the places Natasha lines up for you. It shouldn't take you any longer than a month, maybe two at the most."

"You got it, bro." He reaches across the table, knocking his fist with Aiden's. "When do I leave?"

"I can have Natasha set everything up for you to leave by tomorrow evening. She'll call you with the details as soon as she has it set up." He stuffs a piece of rib in his mouth, closing his eyes with a moan. "Mmm, you're right. These are damn good ribs."

When they finish dinner, Max heads home to prepare for his trip, and Aiden calls Natasha to have her set up his accommodations. He places an ad in the Seattle Times and sets up the company information with a Seattle employment agency. Whether Aiden planned on opening an office across the border or not, it's a venture that's about to take place. This will give him the time he needs to see what Rebecca D'Angelo is all about. Something that can't be done with Max around. Not when he has no intention of sharing her.

Chapter 1 – The Interview

The alarm blasts the new Dua Lipa song levitating, starting the countdown to Rebecca D'Angelo's third and final interview at Collins Enterprises. After accidentally dumping her latte on the CEO, she has no idea how she was even considered for the first interview. There's no doubt in her mind that she ruined his crisp white shirt and Armani suit that day.

Unfortunately, she recalls that morning all too clearly. Rebecca had heard about the account executive position at Collins Enterprises from a friend only a few days prior. With a whopping $75,000 annual base salary up for grabs, she couldn't wait to apply. She put together a stunning portfolio and an impressive résumé, then marched herself directly downtown to the enormous office building.

When she arrived, there was a notice posted on the front door:
DEADLINE - Résumés for the Account Executive position must be received no later than 10 am this morning.

Pulling out her phone, she checked the time— 9:51 am.

Unsure of where she needed to go, she began to panic. She flung open the heavy glass door and darted directly toward the information desk.

At first, she had no idea what she had run into, but it had knocked her clear off her feet. As her portfolio and latte launched into the air, her only thought was, *thank god my documents are in a protective cover.* At least, that was until a set of large hands wrapped around her arms, helping her to her feet. Then, before she could see who it was, his deep voice rumbled next to her ear. "Jesus Christ! This is not a schoolyard, young lady!"

She peered up, her eyes anchoring onto the most gorgeous creature she had ever seen. His beautiful cobalt blue eyes shone like sapphires against a perfect bronze tan, emphasized by neatly combed black hair that flawlessly tapered to meet a designer beard. She could feel the power radiating from his 6' 4" GQ cover body as he wiped her latte from his crisp white dress shirt and expensive Armani suit. There was no mistaking who this man was – Aiden Collins, CEO of Collins Enterprises. Instantly she understood how he earned his status as one of the hottest bachelors in the business sector. Unfortunately, she also understood that she may have just made the biggest mistake of her life.

Shit!

Her hand trembling, she reached out to pick up her portfolio. "I'm so sorry – the deadline," is all she managed to spit out as she stood holding the cheap plastic case in front of her.

He pursed his lips, his eyes narrowing as he extracted the portfolio from her hand. "Yes, well, I'll see that it gets in." Then, turning his back, he walked away without another word.

That's why she's so nervous today – Aiden Collins will be the one conducting her final interview. Yep. That means her fate at Collins Enterprises now lies solely in his hands. On the bright side, she's made it to the third interview regardless of the latte incident. That must say something. Right?

Nervously, she stares at her closet. Okay, the big question – what to wear? If it were up to her, she'd be pulling on a pair of shorts and a tank. After all, what are the odds of her impressing Aiden Collins now? But, on the other hand, she can hear her mother's voice echoing through her mind, *'Honey, no matter what, you must always put your best foot forward.'*

Drawing her shoulders back, she pulls on a black pencil skirt and cream-coloured blouse. "The outfit is for you, momma, but these are for me," she says, slipping her feet into her favourite pair of black stilettos while twirling in front of the full-length mirror. "Now, for this hair."

She combs her mousy blond hair into a high ponytail, adds a little liner and mascara, then shakes her head, frowning in frustration at her reflection. "Too childish," she says, pulling out the tie. Shaking her hair loose, she lets it fall across her shoulders with a groan. "Ugh! Come on, Becca. Which is it going to be, up or down?"

Emma, her roommate and best friend, steps up behind her. She's been watching Rebecca tilt her head from side to side, scrutinizing her appearance from every angle for the past ten minutes. "You need to chill out, Becca. You look great. Very office-e." She scrunches up her face. "You're not planning on wearing that to the bar tonight, though, right?"

Putting her hand on her hip, Rebecca narrows her eyes, drawing a giggle from Emma. "Oh, come on. I'm just joking. Wear what you want, but the only thing that outfit will land you is a stuffy job or an old man." She waves her hand in the air, erasing her last statement. "Anyway, stop fussing. You're going to kill this interview."

Rebecca turns, forcing a smile. "Well, thankfully, I'm not looking for any hot dates right now, but I do want that stuffy job, as you call it."

"Then you're wearing the perfect ensemble," Emma says with a bright smile.

"Thanks for always being so supportive, Em. Truthfully. It means a lot." She glares back into the mirror, pulling her hair up for the fourth time this morning and drops her arms with a huff. "Ah, screw it. Up it is."
Snatching her portfolio and keys from the side table, she takes a deep breath. "Okay. I've gotta run, or I'll be late. Wish me luck."

"Pfft, don't worry. You got this," Em hollers, giving her two thumbs up. "Oh, and for god sake, make sure you skip the latte this morning!"

"Yeah yeah," she says, closing the door.

Rebecca places her portfolio on the passenger seat of her old Mazda and starts the engine. As it sputters to life, she pulls her seatbelt across her chest and takes a quick look into the mirror. Her eyes roam across her face, and for a brief moment, the image of her mother flashes before her. She smiles, raising her hand to her cheek, embracing the fond memory. "Wow. I guess dad's right. I do look like my mom."

Traffic is a little heavier than anticipated. Still, Rebecca's confident that she'll make it there in plenty of time. Finally turning into Collins Enterprises parking lot, she pulls around back and parks under the visitors parking sign. When she steps out of her car, Rebecca takes a minute to gaze up at the largest glass building in Victoria. It's stunning. She can only imagine what the view must be like peering out from the 32nd floor. Catching a glimpse of her reflection on her way inside, she takes a moment to straighten her blouse and push back a stray strand of hair before heading into the impressive lobby.

A short, dignified man with graying hair is standing behind the information desk. He greets her with a broad smile and asks who she'll be seeing. "I'm Rebecca D'Angelo. I have an appointment to meet with Mr. Collins at 11 am."

"Welcome, Miss D'Angelo." He rests his shaky hand on the phone receiver. "Let me just call up and see if Mr. Collins is ready for you."

"Of course. Thank you."

Waiting patiently, Rebecca can't help but wonder if it's Mr. Collins he's speaking to on the other end. Just the thought of seeing him today is making her palms sweat. Finally, having verified her details, the gentleman hands her a visitor's pass and points toward a long corridor. "You'll need to follow the blue dots on the floor to the elevator. Then take it to the 32nd floor and be sure to check in with Natasha at the front desk. You can't miss her. She's the little redheaded beauty as soon as you get off the elevator."

'Ah, so it was his receptionist then,' Rebecca thinks as she thanks him with a smile. Taking the visitor's pass, she starts down the corridor, following the blue dots as he had directed. The butterflies already taking flight as she steps into the elevator and presses the button for the 32nd floor. Taking a deep breath, she steps back as the doors slide closed. Startled by the sudden whoosh as it bounds upward, she grasps the rail and stares up at the numbers as they tick by.

29...30...31...32.

The bell dings, signalling she's reached her destination, and she watches as the doors slowly glide open to a breathtaking view of the city below. Completely lost to the sight before her, she almost misses Natasha's soft voice. "Can I help you, hun?"

Rebecca spins, nervously grasping at her purse strap to save it from hitting the floor as she comes face to face with the beautiful redhead. The gentleman at the information desk wasn't kidding. Natasha is absolutely stunning.

Hating the way her words seem rushed, she can feel her cheeks heat as she blurts out, "Oh, um yes. Forgive me. Rebecca D'Angelo. I have an appointment to see Mr. Collins."

Standing to greet her, Natasha offers her a bright smile. "Of course, Miss D'Angelo. Mr. Collins has been expecting you." Directing her down the hall, she points to the stately wooden door with a nameplate. "It's that second door there on your left. I've been advised to send you right in."

"Thank you." Rebecca clutches her portfolio tightly to her chest as she strides toward his door, stopping just in front to stare up at his nameplate.

Aiden Collins CEO

With her heart racing, she closes her eyes, trying to gain her courage while reciting a mental mantra.
Please, don't let him remember that I was the one who ruined his expensive suit.

Noticing her hesitation, Natasha waves her forward with a flick of her hand. "It's okay, honey. Go on in. He's been expecting you."

Nodding, Rebecca pushes the door open, coming face to face with the man who not so pleasantly wore her latte a mere three weeks earlier.

"Ah, Miss D'Angelo. What a pleasure to see you again. No latte this morning," he asks, waving her in with a slight smirk. "Please" – he fans his hand out to the chair in front of his desk – "make yourself comfortable."

"Thank you. I assure you, Mr. Collins, the pleasure is mine." She hands him her portfolio and takes a seat.
Note to self - Mental mantras officially suck balls!

Butterflies push bile into her throat, and her words come rushing out in a breathless huff. "I'm so sorry about the latte incident, Mr. Collins. I was rushing to—"

Aiden leans forward, raising his hand to stop her. "Whoa whoa whoa, Rebecca. I didn't mean to upset you. My intention was merely to try and break the ice."

Her shoulders relax as he opens her portfolio, flipping

through several pages before his eyes meet hers once again. "It is okay if I call you Rebecca, isn't it," he asks as he closes her portfolio and leans back in his chair.

"Right. I mean, yes, of course. Rebecca's fine. It's my name," she says, fidgeting with a loose string on the cuff of her sleeve.
Shit! Calm down, Becca. He's just a damn man.
A very wealthy, very powerful and incredibly gorgeous man — but he's still just a man.

"Good, and I would prefer it if you call me Aiden." He smiles, undoing the button on his suit jacket. "You seem rather nervous, Rebecca. Do I make you feel uneasy?"

Uneasy? Heck no.
You make my mind take mini-vacations, my heart race, and my panties wet.
But I won't be telling YOU that, now will I, Mr. Collins.
She shakes her head, trying to sound confident. "No—no, I'm fine."

Aiden locks his fingers together, placing his hands on his desk in front of him. "I don't want to beat around the bush with this, Rebecca. Both myself and Mr. Bradley agree that you are the perfect candidate for the account executive position. We would like to bring you on board."

Rebecca tries to suppress the smile fighting to form as she stares down at her fidgeting fingers. Trying to collect herself, she gives him a slight nod. "Thank you, Mr. Collins. I'm very pleased to hear that."
YES!
Oh, hang on. Why am I sensing there's more?

She bites her bottom lip and holds her breath, watching

him stand.

Because there is, Becca, there always is.

That 'more' is quickly confirmed as he walks around to the front of his desk and rests his bottom against it, leaving only inches between them. "Now that we've gotten that out of the way," he says, locking his cobalt blues with hers and letting the slightest smile grace his lips. "I'd like to take you to lunch." His voice carries that air of certainty only he could possess as he calmly leans forward and cups her chin in his hand. "And I thought we agreed you were going to call me Aiden."

Staring into his eyes, she's sure he can see the crimson flood her cheeks as he waits patiently for her response. A bit baffled by this morning's exchange, she swallows hard, praying confidence will resonate in her voice. Though she's sadly disappointed when a barely audible tone leaves her lips. "Lunch?"

His smile slowly broadens as he releases her chin. "Yes, lunch. I'm sure you're able to digest something more nourishing than lattes. You do eat real food, don't you," he asks with a wink.

Straightening in her chair with a nod, she fights the urge to run her hand over her chin, where his hand had just been. "Yes, of course, I eat."

"Great." Aiden stands confidently, refastening his suit coat and adjusts his sleeves. Then, holding her gaze, he picks up the receiver and speaks abruptly to his receptionist. "Natasha, clear my afternoon." Hanging up, he extends his hand toward her with a smile. "Shall we?"

What-the-fuck just happened? Is he really taking me for

lunch?

She stands, reaching for his outstretched hand and clutches her purse in the other. "Uh, sure. I guess lunch would be all right." She glances down at her hand nestled into his palm. It's large but soft, definitely not a hand that has ever seen a hard day's work – that, she's absolutely certain of.

"I'll grab your contract from Natasha on our way out, and you can look it over on our way. We can discuss any discrepancies during lunch." He opens the door, guiding her through, and stops briefly at the reception desk. "Natasha, can you pass me Miss D'Angelo's folder, please?"

The beautiful redhead quickly scurries to the cabinet behind her and hands him a manilla folder. "Here you go, Mr. Collins. I've cleared your afternoon as you've requested, Sir."

He takes it from her hands with a slight nod. "Thank you. Oh, and advise Mr. Bradley, I'll be in touch with him this evening regarding Miss D'Angelo." He places his hand on Rebecca's lower back, guiding her toward the elevator. "Now, what would you like to eat?"

With her mind still whirling from the sudden turn of events, she looks up at him with a glazed-over expression. "I'm not overly picky. I'm sure whatever you choose will be fine."

"Wonderful." A smile graces his face as he pulls out his phone, and his thumbs start flying across the screen.

This is not the Aiden Collins she was prepared to meet today. The man she researched is a demanding hardass – a prick, to say the least. He's a businessman who doesn't like human contact, rarely smiles and always gets what he wants. As far as she can tell, she was already verbally offered the job. Though, verbal isn't a signed contract. She certainly doesn't want to tick him off now by demanding a specific lunch.

She watches Aiden slide his phone back into the breast pocket of his suit coat and press the button for the elevator. As the doors slowly slide open, his hand once again comes to rest on her lower back. He gestures toward the mirrored elevator car. "Beautiful ladies first."

As Rebecca steps into the elevator, she's amazed that she can still feel the heat where his hand had sat on her lower back only moments ago. Never has a man had such an effect on her.

Aiden follows her into the elevator and presses the button for the garage. Her eyes instantly snap up to meet his. "Oh, I parked in visitors parking outback. Could you press the main level for me, please?"

"I see no purpose of taking two vehicles. So we'll take my car, and I'll bring you back here after lunch," he says, closing the topic with no room for debate.

Ah, there he is! There's that demanding Aiden Collins I've read about.
With no room for negotiation, she decides to ask about lunch instead. "Where did you say we're going?"

For a brief moment, she could swear he looks uncomfortable as he shifts his weight and stares up at the floor numbers as they tick by. "Actually, I didn't. However, I thought I'd take you to La Brasserie de Gloutonnerie. Have you been there before?"

She shakes her head in disbelief, glancing down at her office attire before staring back up at him, her face twisted with concern. "No, I haven't, but that's one of the ritziest places in the city. I'm not sure I've dressed appropriately for such a place."

Before she can say anything more, the elevator doors open, and the heat of Aiden's hand guides her out into the garage. Keeping his pace, he leans down, his voice low as it rumbles next to her ear. "Don't be ridiculous. You look amazing."

Every fine hair is instantly called to attention as her shoulders rise – a response to his warm breath brushing over her flesh. He's so close that she wonders if he can hear her heart pounding from his proximity. Extending his hand, he presses the button on his key fob, setting the lights flashing on the sleek black Mercedes directly ahead of them. Quickly stepping out in front of her, Aiden opens the passenger door and waits patiently for her to settle in before walking around to his side. He slides the key into the ignition and pauses, peering over with tight lips. She can feel his stare, but before she can react, he leans over, grabbing the seatbelt and pulls it firmly across her lap to click it into place. "What you do in your vehicle Rebecca, is your business, but everyone buckles up in mine."

Forcing a smile, she places her purse on the floor at her feet. "I'm sorry. I swear, I always wear my seatbelt. I'm not sure where my head is today."

Aiden glances over at her as the engine roars to life. "I wish you'd relax, Rebecca. I'm really not as bad as the articles make me out to be." He places the manilla folder in her lap. "Here are the contracts. You can have a look over them while I drive, and we can discuss any questions or concerns you may have during lunch."

Curious that he has said contracts insinuating there are more than one, she opens the folder and indeed finds two contracts. At first, she thinks nothing of it. Most companies create duplicate copies, one for the company and one for the employee. However, upon closer inspection, she realizes they are entirely different. The first is between Collins Enterprises and herself, as expected, but the second is only between her and Aiden. She turns to face him feeling a little confused. "I'm not sure I understand why I would require a separate contract between you and me."

Peering at her, Aiden graces her with that seemingly ever-present but apparently never to surface smile that everyone speaks of. "Right, well, there is a second offer I'd like you to consider before making your final decision." His voice is calm and confident as his gaze moves back to the road ahead. "Why don't you read through both of them, and we can discuss any of your concerns over lunch."

Her mind giving way to confusion, she finds it difficult to peel her eyes from his beautifully sculpted face. Finally, forcing herself to drag her focus back to the paper in hand, she begins to examine the contract between her and Aiden first.

The initial statements are reasonably standard for a customary agreement. She certainly doesn't see anything that should be cause for alarm. It clearly states that she and Aiden will be entering into a consensual 30-day agreement that will commence upon signing of the contract, blah blah blah. However, when she turns to page 2, where the terms of the agreement are outlined, she feels herself begin to flush.

At a quick glance, she reads terms that immediately alarm her – girlfriend/lover and intimate encounters. Her cheeks heat and she peers over at him, but his confidence hasn't wavered. His focus hasn't moved from the road. Still unsure of what this contract actually consists of, she continues to the summation paragraph.

Summation:
A 30-day exclusive commitment to commence upon signing.
Residency, including shared sleeping accommodation, will be at the Collin's manor (address as stated above) effective immediately.
Intimate affairs/encounters are to be kept exclusive and private.

She pinches her bottom lip.
Oh, my god! This is because of the latte incident. He's still pissed.
This must be a joke – a test. Yes, that has to be it. This is a test.
She glances over at him.
Okay, let's see just how far you're willing to go, Mr. Collins.
She stares back down at the page, continuing from where she had left off.

Aiden Collins will provide all necessary clothing and any personal effects required during the 30-day commitment. Any of these items acquired during the 30-days will be considered gifts.
Full remuneration $300,000.00. The first payment of $150,000.00 upon signing. The final sum of $150,000.00 to be paid on the 31st day. Both to be deposited via bank

transfer.

Furthermore, anything not mutually agreed upon, unless excluded on the opposite side of this contract, will be considered a breach.

Rebecca flips the sheet, quickly glancing at the list on the opposite side. At the top of the page, in big, bold letters, she reads 'Check Strong No's Only.' The page looks similar to a multiple-choice test. There are two columns of checkboxes to the far right of each item. Glancing at the headings, she sees vibrators, oral, nipple stimulation and anal, each with their own subheadings.

Wow, he's certainly not holding back. Of course, if this was real, these things really don't sound so bad — considering we're referring to a man that looks like he just stepped out of a GQ magazine.

She closes her eyes, shaking her head.
Wait—
What if this isn't a joke? I mean, $300,000 could pay off my student loans and buy me a new car.
Christ! I almost want to slap myself for considering such a thing, but I'm honestly torn. I feel the internal tennis match between good and evil at this very moment—my subconscious fighting between desire and disgrace.

Flipping the sheet over, she slumps back against her seat. Her mind whirling at the thought of how to respond. His stare becomes apparent, as does the lack of movement, and she closes the folder, peering over at Aiden. She's unsure how long they've been parked or how long he's been staring at her so intently, but when their eyes meet, her spine tingles. She can feel her vocal cords tighten, and when she opens her mouth, nothing comes out. Aiden seems to read her like a billboard as his deep voice pierces the silence. "You look scared, Rebecca." His voice is low and calm, and oddly enough, the sound of it gently soothes her sudden panic.

Shaking her head, she tries to gain some clarity on the situation. A few questions will need to be asked before agreeing to any contract of this nature, no matter how tempting the financial gain may be. Flexing her vocal cords, she gives her voice another try. "Um, I think shock is a more appropriate word for what I'm feeling. I'm honestly not sure if this is a joke or what it is you're truly asking of me."

Looking a little defeated, Aiden exhales wearily and gives her a nod. "I assure you, it's no joke, Rebecca. Now, I can understand that you may have some concerns. That's why I asked you to lunch. I thought a neutral setting would be more comfortable for this type of discussion." He opens his door, ready to step out and stops for a brief moment. "Stay put. I'll come around to get you."

Aiden steps out of the vehicle and walks around to her side. As he opens her door and extends his hand, flashes erupt around the car. Rebecca looks up at him, shaking her head while mouthing the word 'no' – her hands tight to her chest.

Smiling, he gives her a reassuring nod. "It's okay, Rebecca. I had a feeling you may be a little timid. That's why I parked at the door. Just ignore the photographers. I'm sure they have bigger stories to pursue these days."

When she refuses to take his hand, the muscle in his jaw tenses and his tone deepens. "Rebecca, the longer you take, the more reason you give them to take photos. Now, take my hand and let's go inside."

Her meek and mild manner is suddenly lost somewhere behind the lens of a camera, and her eyes widen with a stubborn glare. "You never mentioned there would be any media here! I haven't agreed to your damn contract yet."

Narrowing his eyes, Aiden leans in with his extended hand, his demands turning to a plea. "Rebecca, please. The door is less than 20 feet away. I'll do my best to shield you from the photographers. Please trust me."

"Fine!" Taking hold of his hand, she leaps from the car, darting for the restaurant's entrance towing him behind.

Once they're safe inside the doors, Aiden drags her to a stop and pulls her tight to his chest. "Whoa, easy, we're inside. Why don't you tell me why you're so upset about the photographers?"

Her first instinct is to shove him away, but the goosebumps erupting over her skin as she smells his cologne, and the safety of his embrace says otherwise. Conflicted, she steps back to look into his eyes. Now with some distance between them, her anger begins to resurface. He has no right to put her in this position. "What if I disagree with your contract? Then those pictures today would label me as one of your playboy conquests. I've seen your Google photo album, Mr. Collins. Although it's quite an impressive spread, I don't care to be part of it."

A smirk forms on his lips as he brushes a stray hair from her face. "There's a simple solution for that concern, Rebecca. Sign the contract. Instead of a conquest, as you call it, you'll be my girlfriend. You've clearly read the articles.

You must know I've never been seen with any woman more than once."

Anger flashes through her like a lightning bolt. Before she realizes what has happened – she punches him in the face. "You're an arrogant asshole!"

Cradling her hand to her chest as the pain shoots through her knuckles, Rebecca watches as Aiden rubs his hand along his jaw, moving it from right to left. From the look on his face, it's quite evident that he's angry, but as soon as his eyes fall to her hand, his demeanour shifts.

"Shit! Are you okay?" He reaches for her hand, carefully pulling it toward him. Placing a light kiss on her throbbing knuckles, he smiles down at her. "Well, the good news is that you can move your fingers. My best guess is that it's not broken. Why don't I get you some ice?"

Pursing her lips, she shakes her head. "No, I'm fine."

His tone softens as he pulls her into his chest. "I'm sorry, Rebecca. I suppose I deserved that. I'm used to dealing with a different breed of women. That much you are right about."

She pulls out of his arms and peers up. "Yes, you did deserve that. I don't care who you are," she says, clenching her teeth. "Not even you, Mr. Collins, is allowed to put me on the spot like that." With her temper threatening to resurface, she turns to leave.

Aiden reaches for her arm. "Look, I said I was sorry," he says, spinning her back to face him. "Sometimes, I don't think before I speak. Please, forgive me. I'll take care of any photos that may have been taken. A table has been set up on the rooftop for us. There are no photographers up there, and we can talk privately about any other concerns you may have with the contract. Can we please just go have a nice lunch?" His eyes wildly scan her face for a reaction before he slowly releases her, putting his hands up in front of him in defence. "Just lunch and a private conversation. For the record, I've mentally noted – no more unannounced media. I promise."

As the fog begins to clear and the adrenaline subsides, it finally dawns on her –
Oh my god! I just punched Aiden Collins in the jaw! Holy shit!

Noticing his defensive stance, Rebecca shakes her head, offering a slight smile. "I'm sorry. Maybe I shouldn't have punched you," she says meekly, somewhat returning to the young lady that walked into his office this morning. "I'm not usually a violent person."

He runs his hand over his jaw as the corner of his mouth lifts into a half-smile. "It's okay. You're right. I did deserve that." His upper body jerks with amusement as he laughs. "For a little lady, you have quite the right hook. I'll definitely try to use a little more tact in the future."

Chapter 2 — Lunch

Rebecca bows her head, trying to hide her crimson cheeks as she follows him through the kitchen to the elevator. Stopping abruptly, Aiden leans in close to her ear. "I'm almost afraid to ask, but are you okay with rib-eye? I pre-ordered for us, but I can change the order before we go up to the rooftop if you'd prefer something else."

A smirk pulls at her lips, and she tucks her chin to her chest to conceal it as she shakes her head. "No, rib-eye is a wonderful choice. Thank you for asking."

As the elevator reaches the rooftop, the doors slide open, and a waiter in a tuxedo is standing on the other side with a wide smile. "Good afternoon, Mr. Collins." He bows his head slightly toward Rebecca. "Good afternoon, madam."

Aiden places his hand on her lower back, guiding her toward the lone table and addresses the waiter. "I've pre-ordered our meal with the chef. Would you let him know we're here, please?"

Pouring each of them a glass of champagne, he glances up, "Certainly, Sir. Then, with a slight bow, he exits toward the elevator.

Leaning back in her chair, Rebecca toys with the stem on her champagne glass, taking a moment to observe this man across from her. A man who has requested 30 days with her at a price – a very high price. For the life of her, she can't understand why. He is the epitome of masculinity. The aura of authority that ripples off this man is apparent. People seem to jump to attention when they're in his presence. They beg to be near him—to have his approval. She's sure he could have anyone he wanted. So why her?

The moment the elevator door closes and they are alone, she can feel his stare. His deep voice dances across the crystal, reaching her ears like a song. "So, do tell me, Rebecca. What is it that concerns you most about the contract?"

She takes a sip of her champagne, contemplating the unusual proposal, then tips her head with a raised brow. "Well, honestly, it's the entire thing. If you're asking me to be your live-in sex toy for the next 30 days, then I'm afraid you have the wrong lady, Mr. Collins. I'm not an escort."

Trying to digest her words, Aiden nearly chokes on his champagne. Finally, he sets his glass down and glances up, dabbing his mouth with his napkin. He closes his eyes and takes a deep breath, releasing it slowly before responding. "Not at all, Rebecca. The last thing I would consider you to be is an escort. That is certainly not what I'm asking for unless, of course, that's what you're offering." He shifts in his seat, his voice rising as he continues. "I have no problem adjusting the contract, and for god's sake, I thought we agreed you'd call me Aiden."

As Rebecca's mouth falls open, a sly smirk works across his face. "Look, let's be honest, I could hire an escort for far less than I'm offering you for 30 days of your undivided attention. So please, don't devalue yourself or insult me with such nonsense."

"But you want my sexual preferences, and it clearly says I'd be sharing your bed," she blurts out, meeting his stare.

"True," he says, picking up his spoon and turning it over in his fingers as he leans back in his chair. "Let me try to be as transparent as I can. I'm 29 years old, Rebecca. It's time for me to settle down." Briefly glancing at her, he tilts his head. "You're a smart young lady. I know you've done your homework just as well as I have. Can you picture the type of women that are in my phone book?" She scrunches her nose, looking down at her glass to avoid his gaze. "Exactly. Not quite the type of women you'd consider a sincere relationship with." Shrugging, his spoon stills in his hands. "I'll be honest. I'm rather drawn to you. I guess one could say you've awakened some part of my inner senses." He sets his spoon down and reaches for his glass. "I find you very attractive and naturally wholesome. I've personally been observing you since the day you introduced me to your latte" – he smiles – "and I very much like what I've seen."

A sick feeling washes over her. "Wait. You've been stalking me?" She's about ready to leave when Aiden's big hand reaches across the table to rest on hers. It's not a feeling she can explain, but it brings an instant calm, and her body begins to relax.

His eyes soften as the corners of his mouth tug upward. "No. I wouldn't exactly call it stalking, more like observing. Besides, it's not uncommon for us to check out anyone we're considering bringing on board. You'd be amazed at the double lives some people lead – some that include illicit drugs and violence. Not to mention, some are thieves and reporters looking for the inside story. So we must be careful who we choose to have publicly associated with Collins Enterprises."

Aiden releases her hands as the waiter brings out their food. His tone deepens as he squints up to address him. "Thank you. Could you please ensure that we're not disturbed any further?"

"Of course, Sir. There's a doorbell beside the door. Just ring if you require anything," he says, giving a slight bow as he backs away.

Peering down into her empty champagne glass, Rebecca watches him leave. She had assumed the waiter was going to refill their glasses when he had brought dinner. Shrugging, she reaches for the bottle. Aiden's hand covers hers. "Forgive me. I wasn't paying attention." His radiant blue eyes meet hers as he takes the bottle from her hand. "Now, as I was trying to explain. The contract is merely an outline of our relationship expectations."

Relationship?
Her brows draw together as she shakes her head. "Wait, you think this is the way to ask someone to start dating? You know this is not the typical way it's done in my world, right?"

He shrugs with an uncommitted nod. "Yes, well, per se. We'd be entering into a relationship on a 30-day trial basis."

What – the – fuck? He cannot be serious. What world is this guy from?
I'm beginning to think I should be looking for a hidden camera or expecting someone to jump out yelling, 'you've been

punked!'

Setting his fork down across his plate, Aiden places his hands on the table in front of him. Intertwining his fingers together, he peers directly into her eyes. "Rebecca, this contract will ensure both of our needs are satisfied. Think of it as a prenuptial of sorts" – he shrugs – "without the nuptials."

Rebecca's jaw drops as she glances around the rooftop. "What? You're joking, right? Is someone going to come out now and yell, gotcha?"

Shaking his head, he reaches for her hands, holding them snugly in his. "No, Rebecca. This is not a joke. Look, think of it as a trial period to see if I can live with you, if you can live with me – if we enjoy each other. To see if we can compromise, work things out together." He locks his pleading blues with hers and asks, "You wouldn't buy a car without test driving it, would you?"

Her eyes grow wide, and she can feel her face begin to burn. "Christ! Did you seriously just say that," she asks. Narrowing her eyes, she shakes her head. "I mean, you did not just compare dating me to buying a damn car, right?" Still seething, she tries to pull free of his hands only to have him tighten his grip.

Slowly shaking his head, he lifts his index finger. "Oh no, there will be no more hitting. Look, I apologize. I may have worded that incorrectly. As you may have noticed, I'm not very good at this sort of thing. I've never considered a relationship before I met you. What I meant is, we should be able to tell within the next 30 days if we are compatible for something more long-term." He carefully releases her hands and leans back in his chair, jabbing his hand through his hair. "Jesus, this is not exactly going the way I had expected it to."

"Oh, and what exactly did you expect, Aiden? Did you expect that I would just sign the contract, and we'd go back to your place to fuck like wild animals? I mean, this isn't exactly what I was expecting today either."

Aiden's eyes grow wide at her brazen statement. This is not the wholesome young lady he's been observing for the past three weeks. "Now this" – he fans his hands out in front of him – "this is the reason contracts exist. The expectations are outlined, leaving no room for this kind of misconception." He downs his champagne and peers into her eyes. "Look, let me be completely honest with you. I have never had a real relationship before. Hell, I've never even considered one. Why Rebecca? – Because – I – know – contracts. Not relationships! I have honestly never been with a woman for longer than a quick evening of mutual satisfaction in the past. Oh, and for the record, I hadn't planned on jumping straight into sex, but hell" – he throws his hands up and leans back in his chair, shaking his head – "if you're that damn adamant about it. I'm certainly not going to say no. We can fuck like any damn animal you choose."

His outburst is entirely out of character for the all-mighty Aiden Collins, but it's kind of friggin' cute. She truly almost feels bad for making him upset. "Okay okay, I'm sorry. I may have taken that a bit far." She takes his hand. "Let me be sure that I understand. The contract merely states that we'll be dating and that I can't tell the press about any of our intimate moments. Is that right?"

A lopsided grin begins to form across his lips as his breathing calms, and he contemplates his answer. "Yes, in a manner of speaking, that's correct."

The tension that releases from his shoulders as he says 'Yes' is almost palpable.

Ah, shit! He thinks he's just closed the deal.
Oh, you might be gorgeous, Mr. Collins, but I'm not quite that easy.
She tosses that statement around in her mind for a brief moment.
Oh, who the hell am I kidding?
I guess I am –
I don't need any damn contract to date him!
I have dreamt of having sex with him—many, many times.
I could care less if this only lasts for 30 days. I just wish this wasn't the way he asked.

Her mouth suddenly feels as dry as the Sahara desert. She reaches for her champagne, hoping merely to quench her thirst, but instead, she inadvertently gulps the remaining half glass. A bit stunned by her own actions, she calmly sets her champagne flute down and looks up at Aiden. As she squints against the afternoon sun, the lightning rod behind him causes her to take a second look.
Is that a blivet?
Whoa!
Thankfully I'm not superstitious cause nothing flashes warning like a devil's pitchfork.

A giggle escapes her, and she throws her hand over her mouth. "Oh, I'm sorry. I think I may have exceeded my limit of champagne," she says, still smiling, as she sets her glass down.

The sweet sound of Aiden's laugh graces her ears, and instantly any residual tension at the table dissipates. He waves off her apology. "Don't be silly. Your smile is contagious." He gestures to her plate. "Are you ready for dessert?"

"Actually, what I really want is Dippin' Dots ice cream from the harbour. I can always make room for that."

"All right," he says with a curt nod. "I can make that happen. I guess we're ready then?" Rebecca places her napkin on the table, and he stands. "Okay. We just need to ring for the waiter."

Aiden takes her by the hand, leading her toward the door to buzz the bell. It isn't more than a few minutes before the door springs open, and the waiter promptly steps through, looking a little surprised to see them both waiting by the door. "Is everything all right, Sir?"

"Oh yes, everything was perfect as usual. However, we've decided to skip dessert. I gave my card to the chef when I ordered earlier. Just be sure to add an appropriate tip for yourself."

"Thank you very much, Mr. Collins," he replies, holding the elevator door open while they enter the car. "Thanks for dining at La Brasserie de Gloutonnerie. I hope you enjoy the rest of your day."

"Thank you," Rebecca says as Aiden presses the button for the kitchen, and the elevator doors slide closed.

Standing next to her, he leans down and inhales next to her hair. "I must say, Rebecca, you do smell absolutely divine." A slight smirk emerges on his face as he watches the crimson fill her cheeks. Now that she's returned to her mild-mannered self, it's difficult to believe she's the same little wildfire that punched him in the jaw only hours ago. When the elevator comes to a halt, and the doors glide open, he extends his elbow. "Well, Miss D'Angelo, shall we get some ice cream?"

Smiling, she slides her arm through his. "Absolutely, we shall, Mr. Collins."

Leading her toward the rear of the kitchen, Aiden gestures toward the backdoor. "I thought you might prefer it if we snuck out the back to avoid any photographers."

"That's very thoughtful. Thank you. I don't care to be seen within the pages of your portfolio. I'm sorry if that's a deal-breaker." She looks up at him with an exaggerated smile and shakes her head. "I've never cared much for the media, and besides, I'm not a very photogenic person."

"Oh, I beg to differ, Rebecca. You're a lovely young lady," he says, folding his hand over hers as it rests in the crease of his arm.

Of course, she's quite sure that her little scene out front had something to do with him having valet park his car in the rear. Still, she's grateful, even if it is because he doesn't want his reputation tarnished with photos of an unwilling young lady.

As they reach the rear parking lot, she inhales deeply, taking in the refreshing ocean air. She's always loved the Inner Harbour. The statues and gardens are incredible, and the walkways are never lacking diverse entertainment. She peers up at him with pleading eyes. "It's such a beautiful day, and the Harbour is only across the street. Do you think we can walk across?"

"Of course we can. Just let me leave my jacket and tie in the car." Aiden undoes his jacket and hangs it from a hook in the backseat, then loosens his tie and pulls it over his head. Then, turning around to face her, he opens the top two buttons on his shirt and stills, his eyes fixed on hers as they trail across his body.

Everything seems to disappear around her as Rebecca watches Aiden discard his jacket and tie. She can't believe just how exquisite this man really is. Her eyes slowly scan the length of his body while her mind takes note of every visible feature.
Damn, bless that crisp white shirt for fitting so snugly. I love the way it shows every sculpted muscle of his chest and biceps as it tapers down to his waist. And that dark hair, I have an incredible urge to run my hand through those gorgeous dark locks that never seem to be out of place — and to feel that well-kept stubble that flawlessly graces his jawline. I wonder if it's really as soft as it looks.
My god! He just licked his lips! I swear I just soaked my panties. Those full and oh so sinfully tempting lips. Damn, what I would give to taste them. Oh, and those eyes, mesmerizing cobalt blue eyes that scream for your attention.
Ah, shit!
Shit shit shit! Those beautiful blues that are staring back at me right now.

As if he can read her thoughts, he holds out his hand with a smug smile. "Are you ready?"

Closing her eyes, Rebecca takes a deep breath and clenches her legs, trying to quell the crazy twitch between her thighs. Smiling, she nods. "Uh, yeah. I'm ready."

His eyes shift from her tightened thighs back up to meet hers as he raises his brow. "Do you need to use the restroom before we go?"

Heat creeps across her cheeks as she grabs his arm with a giggle and tugs him forward. "No no, I'm good. Let's go."

Casually strolling along the Causeway at the Inner Harbour, they stop every so often to hear a musician or watch an artist at work. When they finally reach the steps leading up to Belleville St., Rebecca spots the Dippin' Dots cart selling the best ice cream pellets ever made. They take their cups of tiny beaded ice cream treats and sit down on the grass overlooking the ocean.

As she lets the tiny beads of ice cream melt in her mouth, Rebecca starts to think about their lunch date.

All in all, if this were a 'real' date — it would be perfect. Almost. I mean, minus the indecent proposal and the punch to the jaw. Oh, and I guess there's the whole comparing dating me to test driving a car.

Okay, never mind, maybe it's not such a perfect date after all, but it hasn't been a total nightmare.

She glances over at Aiden. He's propped up on his elbow, picking at the grass while he waits for her to finish her ice cream. His agitation becomes apparent as he starts to pick small handfuls of the turf and toss them aside instead of single blades. Then, like the true acquisition hunter he is, he looks over at her, squinting his eyes in question. "Rebecca, I have to ask. Are you giving the contract any consideration?"

Her head falls to her shoulder as she rolls her eyes. Swallowing what she has in her mouth, she clears her throat and peers at him out of the corner of her eye. "Aiden, do you honestly need an answer today? I'd like to have a better look at it before I commit myself." Finishing off her ice cream, she discards the dish in the trash beside her.

He sits up, draping his arms across his knees with a smile. "I'm not surprised that you want a couple of days to think it over. In fact, I'd worry if you didn't." Standing, he brushes himself off. "Take a couple of days and think about it. Why don't we meet at my office Friday at 10 am? That gives you a couple of days to mull it over. How's that sound?"

If I could do it without drawing attention, I'd pat myself on the back. I've successfully stalled the King of Guaranteed 1st Proposal Closers.
That's huge!
Trying to keep her composure, she squints against the sun, nodding with a slight smile. "Okay, that sounds fair."

"Yes," he laughs sardonically. "I have to say that's more than fair," he says, suddenly sounding all businesslike again. "But I want you to know that I'll expect solid reasoning for anything you may disagree with. You see, Rebecca, I'm aware that my offer is quite generous. So, be sure you give it the consideration it deserves." He holds his hand out. "Come on. I'll take you back."

Once Rebecca settles into the passenger seat, she immediately goes back to examining the contracts. He's pleased that she's eager to get back to them, but it's probably best if she does that when she's at home on her own. Besides, her mind is currently on *their* contract, and that's where he wants to keep it. They can talk business any time. He gently lays his hand over hers, closing the folder. "Why don't you go over them when you get home? My cell number is at the top. You can always call me if you have any further questions or concerns."

Her smile is so sweet. It screams innocence as she shyly nods with a barely audible, "Okay."

Rebecca has her gaze fixed out the window as they drive back to the office, and fortunately, she does. When she looks over at Aiden, he seems to be too busy watching her to notice he's missed their turn.

God, how many times in the last three weeks have I thought about those toned thighs wrapped around my head? Her ample breasts in my mouth –

"Um, Aiden. We just passed the office," she says, quietly drawing him back from his dirty little daydream.

"Shit!" He shakes his head, pulling into the next driveway to turn around. "I must have gotten lost in your beauty." He can't help but smile as she dips her head, trying to hide the flush that works across her cheeks.

Rebecca points toward the back of the parking lot, directing him toward her car. Sure enough, it's still parked in the exact place where he had seen it as they had driven by earlier. He looks at the offensive little car that should be in its new home at the scrapyard by now and cringes.
God damn it! I told Natasha to have that piece of shit towed. Obviously, they haven't gotten here yet. Now I'm going to need a new angle to be able to drive her home. I was hoping to be her chauffeur until I can convince her to sign the contract.

She points toward the old blue Mazda. "I'm the little blue

one there at the back."

He glances at her as if she's crazy, slowing down alongside it, but he refuses to stop. "Rebecca, that car should not be on the road. When I saw it earlier, I messaged Natasha and asked her to have it towed. I thought someone left their scrap here. I'm surprised they haven't been by to pick it up yet." The look on her face is one of pure shock. For a moment, he wonders if he should protect his face from another fist. "Look, don't worry. I'll drive you home tonight, and I'll get you a new car in the morning."

Rebecca turns to glare at him. "What? You knew that was my car! You've been bloody following me! You even told me so!"

He takes a deep breath placing his hands in the air defensively. "No, well, yes – I did know it was your car, but it's not safe. Let's be honest. You don't need that specific car. You just need a car. That car is a death trap, Rebecca."

"You can't just buy me a new car! I haven't agreed to *either* contract yet." Her glare slices through him like a scalpel as her hands ball into fists in her lap. "Aiden, stop! I'm not joking. Crappy or not, I need my car!"

Stopping at the edge of the parking lot, he turns to face her. "Look, I said I would buy you a new car – a safe one. I promise Rebecca, no strings attached. You can consider it a gift. It'll be a tax write-off for me."

She flings her head back against the headrest and looks over at him. "Aargh! You can't be serious? Do you have any idea how frustrating you can be? I'm supposed to be meeting my roommate at the Purple Lion at eight o'clock tonight. I don't know anything about the buses in this city, and cabs cost a fortune."

Perfect! Another opportunity to spend some time with her.
He reaches for her hand and runs his thumb across the top, marvelling at the softness of her skin. "Rebecca, please, you can trust me. I will even take you to meet your friend myself. I can pick you up at seven-thirty and take you."

Her head jolts up as she peers at him through wild eyes. "What?"

"I said, I'll take you. You said the Purple Lion, right? I know where it is. That's no problem."
I've never been inside before, but I've followed her home from the place several times in the past three weeks.

She bursts out laughing, and even she can't miss the cynical ring it carries. "You want to take me to the Purple Lion?" Aiden nods confidently. "You do know there are no crystal goblets or fine china there, right?"

He can't help but smirk at her thoughts of him. Sure he enjoys the finer things in life. Though when he's not in the public eye, he's just your average guy.
I want so badly to show her the real Aiden Collins. The one that enjoys life has a dangerous side and loves to break free from the suits and high society. I want to introduce her to the Aiden that wants to own her – body and mind, even if it is only for a short time.

Rebecca clenches her teeth, unsure of how to make him understand. Finally, she takes a deep breath and tries one last time. "Aiden, let me help you comprehend. People don't wear suits or drink champagne there!"

Ohh, she is a brazen little vixen. He raises his brow, fighting to retain his composure. "Rebecca, please. Will you trust me not to embarrass you? I'm trying to show you I can be accommodating and flexible. I'm not completely as I may seem on the exterior. You know, I do happen to own a pair of jeans and a t-shirt."

Deflating into her seat, she huffs. "I'm not afraid you'll embarrass me. I just think it's completely out of your element, but if you feel you're up to it. I'll be ready for seven-thirty."

"Great!" He pulls into her driveway and shifts the car into park. As he turns to face her with a broad smile, he reaches out to take her hand. "Then, I'll be back to pick you up at seven-thirty." He lifts her hand to his lips and lightly brushes a kiss over the very same knuckles that grazed his jaw earlier. "I only have one condition." He lowers his head, looking at her through his brows. "You must promise there will be no more hitting."

"I promise not to slug you if you promise not to treat me like one of your tramps," she says cocking her head with a smirk.

Lifting his head, he scans her face for a brief moment, the corner of his mouth tugging upward to mimic hers. *This girl is certainly nothing like the women I've dated in the past. She has a mind of her own and a feisty little spirit.* "Rebecca, I'm fully aware you're not a tramp. I promise to be on my best behaviour, and I expect that you will be too."

Pursing her lips, she gives him a slight nod. "Okay then, I guess I'll see you at seven-thirty." Without another word, she steps out of the car and saunters up the walkway disappearing into the house.

Chapter 3 — Skinny Dippin'

It's already 6 pm when Aiden arrives home. He knows he still has a twenty-minute drive back to Rebecca's. So, he takes a quick shower and trims away any stray facial hair, then heads for his closet to find something to wear. Pulling on his favourite pair of distressed blue jeans, he lets them ride low on his hips then grabs a new white Henley from the hanger. It's a bit snug, but he likes the feel and how it shows the defined muscles underneath. He takes a quick look in the mirror, running his hands through his hair and lets it settle naturally. Splashing on some cologne, he admires the laid-back casual look. It's just the right image he wants to share tonight. Rebecca needs to see that he's more than just a tight-ass in a designer suit. Tonight, that small piece of the Aiden Collins he never shares with anyone is taking her out.

He looks over at the clock – 7:05 pm. "Shit!" Grabbing his keys, he heads for the door.

On his drive back to Rebecca's house, he fidgets with the radio, trying to decide what music he should have on. Stumbling across a country station, he laughs to himself. "Okay, next. I'm fairly certain country isn't her jam." Flipping the channel again, he hears a familiar song by Leona Lewis and decides to leave it. "Now, this sounds more like her style."

Pulling into Rebecca's driveway, he's quite pleased when he looks at the clock. It's seven-thirty on the button. Generally, he would bring flowers, but he doesn't want to push her. He wants her to believe he's doing this as a favour, not that this is a date.

He steps out of his car, brushing his hands down his chest as though his shirt might wrinkle, then casually strolls up the walkway to her door and rings the bell. When she opens the door, Aiden suddenly remembers why he's pursuing her while his brother's out of town. Max would be on her like a fat kid on cake. In fact, he regrets mentioning her to him at all.

He steps back, taking a good look at the young lady he'll be accompanying tonight.
Christ, she's breathtakingly beautiful. I love her hair down. It makes me want to run my hands through those soft curls. The way they frame her face highlights her cheekbones and those dark, sensual eyes.
He wets his lips, his eyes carrying down her frame.
That black spandex dress leaves barely anything to the imagination—showing off every perfect little curve right down to the slight dip of her belly button. Mmm, and she's wearing those signature black stilettos. God, how I've come to love those shoes. The way they lengthen her legs, making them scream for attention.

"Wow," she says, breaking through his thoughts as she nods her approval. "I must say, I rather like the dressed-down Aiden."

Tucking his hand into the front pocket of his jeans, he tips his head with a slight smile. "Well, thank you, Miss D'Angelo. You look rather stunning yourself. I suppose there's no chance you might have considered signing that contract while I've been gone, hmm?"

She fumbles with the lock on the door, trying desperately to conceal her smile. "I believe we had agreed you were going to give me a couple of days to think it over. Friday morning was the deadline, wasn't it?"

"Yes, of course. I just thought you may have come to a decision sooner." Aiden places his arm around her and tucks her into his side with an adoring squeeze. "In my business, I've learned that the answer will always be no if you don't ask."

He reaches out in front of her and opens the car door, waiting for her to settle in before closing it and walking around to the driver's side. As he takes his seat, he looks over and admires the long locks draped over her shoulders. Then, unable to resist the urge any longer, he wraps a long tendril of her hair around his finger, closing his eyes as he savours the softness.
God, it's even softer than I had imagined.
"Your hair looks lovely, Rebecca. You should consider wearing it down more often."

Heat quickly radiates through her cheeks as she drops her gaze to her lap, pretending to fidget with the hem of her dress. "Thanks." Peeking over at him through the corner of her eye, she smiles. "You look like less of a tight-ass in jeans. You should consider wearing *them* more often."

Aiden can never seem to read this girl – she's one big surprise. The sound of sweet and sassy is all wrapped up in one beautiful little bundle. He loves it. You never really know what you're going to get – that sassy hot-headed edge or that meek, mild-mannered side. Nevertheless, this new double banger of sweet and sassy in one mouthful makes his manhood swell against his jeans. He's definitely going to have to keep her away from Max.

Shifting the car into gear, he glances over with a smirk. "Thanks, I'll try to keep that in mind."

They're almost halfway to the Purple Lion when the song 34 + 35 by Ariana Grande comes on the radio. He hears Rebecca singing and glances over to see her head swaying and her finger tapping on her thigh. Pleased to see she's finally relaxed back into the young lady he's been observing these past few weeks, he turns his attention back to the road, tapping his fingers on the steering wheel to the beat.

Rebecca sits forward, staring at the full parking lot as they drive up to the Purple Lion. "Hmm, that's odd. I wonder who's playing tonight. I don't recall seeing it this busy before."

Aiden pulls into the bistro parking lot across the road and stares out the windshield at the lineup out front of the bar. "If we can't get in, I'd be happy to take you somewhere else. I mean, we're already out, and you look fantastic. I see no reason why we shouldn't enjoy our evening."

"Oh, I'm not worried about getting in. My roommate Emma works here. We'll get in." She points to the crowd waiting outside the door. "Don't let that line-up bother you. We won't be standing in that."

Rebecca reaches for his hand, pulling him toward the door, but as they approach the edge of the parking lot - she freezes. Her face drops, and her body tenses. "Oh shit!"

Her voice suddenly trails off to a weak mumble. "That's Alex and his band. Emma didn't mention they were playing here tonight."

"What? What is it? Are you all right," Aiden asks, turning her to face him. "You look a little pale. If you're not comfortable being here, we don't have to stay."

She stares up at him nervously, her eyes almost pleading. "Okay, Aiden. I'll spend the next 30 days with you. I promise I'll sign the contract as soon as I get home."

"Whoa, wait a minute. What have I missed?" Her sudden shift hits him off guard. Taking a step back, he studies this suddenly panicked young lady in front of him. As much as he wants to claim victory, he'd like to know what source is generating this rash decision. "Look, I'm ecstatic that you're suddenly willing to sign on the dotted line, but it does raise the question of what has caused this sudden change of heart."

Her nostrils flare as she tenses her jaw. "Jesus, Aiden! Are you going to accept my verbal signature or not?"

Stepping back, Aiden folds his arms, contemplating her sudden change in demeanour.
Oh, she's a snappy little thing when she wants to be.
Is she really trying to play hardball with me right now?
Me, Aiden Collins?

He runs his hand along the stubble on his chin, trying to contain his smile.
I do kind of like this feisty side of her.
Hell yeah, we can play ball, Rebecca!
But, if we're going to play, we're going to play my way.
Game on. Let's play ball!

"Rebecca, you know a verbal signature will never do. If you're serious—" He pulls out his phone, scanning through his files until he finds a copy of the contract and hands it to her. "Here, just sign it."
He pulls his phone back briefly and reminds her that this is indeed an actual contract. "I want you to bear in mind that there is no turning back once it's signed – this is not a joke. The terms of the contract will be effective immediately. That means you will leave here tonight with me."
It would be foolish to try to talk her out of signing it, but I'm not a total prick. I do want to be sure she understands the end result.

She bounces anxiously on the balls of her feet, snatching the phone from his hand. "I'm not a child Aiden. I completely understand how contracts work."

His eyes widen, and he folds his arms with a smile as he watches her shakey hand sign her name across his phone. *Ah yes, there it is. Finally, she's mine! At least for the next 30 days, she's all fucking mine!*

She hands him back his phone with a sigh of relief that mystifies him. "There, now we're officially dating, right?"

Aiden peers down at her signature, his smile slowly broadening. "Yes – Contractually speaking. It's official," he says, tucking his phone into his pocket. "Now, would you care to explain what caused your sudden change of heart?"

Shaking her head, she pulls him forward and continues toward the door. "I'm sure you'll understand soon enough."

As soon as the doorman Randy spots Rebecca, he gives her a wink. "Hey, Becca! Looking good, baby girl." He studies Aiden for a brief minute then realizes who he is. "Oh shit. Hey, Mr. Collins! Welcome to the Purple Lion!"

Aiden is still focused on Rebecca's sudden change of heart and the probability that someone at this club may have caused it. He gives him a quick nod, barely acknowledging him and protectively tucks her in close to his side. "Yeah, thanks."

Searching the crowd, Rebecca looks back up at the doorman. "Hey Randy, have you seen Emma?"

"Sure, sweet thing." He points toward the large table directly off to the side of the stage. "She's down at the back." Leaning in a little closer, he skeptically eyes Aiden. "Hey, um, Alex has been asking for you since he got here."

She pats his arm, giving him a tight-lipped smile. "Great. Thanks, Randy. I'll catch you later."

Alex, huh? I think it's safe to assume he's the reason for the sudden change of heart.
Aiden gives Randy a curt nod as Rebecca takes his hand, leading him through the doors.

The band is good. In fact, Aiden recognizes them from the radio. He can certainly understand how they could draw a fair-sized crowd. Rebecca suddenly comes to a dead stop and is staring up at the stage. She has a glazed-over look. Maybe she's fan-struck or lost in the music. He studies her for a few more seconds.

Shit!
Nope, it has nothing to do with the music, and I don't believe

that's a fan's response.
I've seen that look on women before - that's hurt.

Aiden steps up next to her and presses his lips against her ear. "Rebecca, I'm not sure what the story is with you and that singer, but you can take refuge in me. Just tell me what you need."

As he steps back, she looks up at him, trying to blink away the tears as they start to pool in her eyes. "Kiss me. Please. I just need you to kiss me, Aiden."

He might be a little taken back by her request, but he doesn't hesitate to respond. Licking his lips, he slides his hand under her hair and grips the nape of her neck. Rebecca closes her eyes, melting against him as he leans down, gently pressing his lips to hers. When her arms wrap around him, his tongue slides past her lips, sweeping away all her dilemmas. The tension that had consumed her body only moments ago – gone. Leaning back slightly, he lifts her chin with his finger and peers into her eyes. "Your lips are even sweeter than I had imagined."

Quickly dropping her eyes from his, the slightest of a smile plays on her lips. "That was *exactly* as I have imagined."

Turning toward Emma's table, Rebecca takes a deep breath as she watches her stand with her mouth agape, flailing her arms in the air. "Well, this should be an interesting conversation," she says, heading in her direction. "I think I'll let you explain. After all, it was your idea to bring me here, and well, we are dating now."

Aiden smirks, waving his finger. "Yes, but that kiss though, that was your idea." Stopping, she glances over at him, her cheeks gaining the slightest tinge of pink. He raises his hands with a smile. "Oh, that's not a complaint. In fact" – he pulls her to his chest – "I have no issue with repeating that kiss right now."

Giggling, she slides out of his arms. "Come on, I'm still trying to recover from the last one."

As they approach the table, Emma stands to give Rebecca a hug. She grasps her shoulders, keeping her at arm's length as she shakes her head. "Wow, Becca! I can't believe you brought Aiden fucking Collins to the Purple Lion!"

Smiling, Rebecca ignores her comment and takes Aiden's hand. "Emma, as I'm sure you know, this is Aiden Collins. Aiden, this is my roommate and best friend, Emma."

Emma flicks her finger back and forth between the two of them. Her eyes lock onto Rebecca's as her brow lifts. "Wait a minute. Is this a date? Are you two dating?"

Rebecca opens her mouth as if she's about to answer when Aiden clears his throat. Trying to hide her smile, she shifts her gaze back to Emma. She can't wait to see her reaction.

Okay, let's see what wonderfully crafty tale you have, Mr. Collins. Surely, it won't contain a contract.

He puts his arm around Rebecca, tucking her into his side and graces Emma with a bright smile. "Yes, I suppose you could say this is a date." He glances down at Rebecca. "And yes, I'm sure it all appears a bit odd, but I haven't been able to take my mind off of her since that first day we met in my lobby. We've spent our day together, and we've decided we're much more compatible on a personal level than on a business one. Isn't that right, Rebecca?"

Stunned at how quickly he spits that spiel out, she smiles up at him and nods. "Mmhmm, I couldn't have said it better myself."

She bounces up on her toes, kissing him lightly on his cheek. "I would never have guessed it myself, but then here we are," she declares, snuggling into his side.

Cocking her head, Emma stares at Aiden. "You mean since she dumped her latte all over you and ruined your Gucci suit," she says matter-of-factly.

The corner of Aiden's mouth tightens as he gives her a confirming nod. "Actually, it was an Armani, but yes. That would be the day."

Still a bit skeptical, she sits back down and studies them both for a moment. Her face slowly works into a smile as her eyes shift back to Aiden. "Well shit, Aiden, I kind of like you." She gestures to the empty chairs on the opposite side of the table. "Well, what are you two waiting for? Have a seat." She leans over the table, cranking her finger at Rebecca. "I'm not sure if you're going to like this, but Alex has been waiting to see you. He's due for a break anytime now."

Rebecca glances over at Aiden. "Right, well, I'm not sure if we're going to stay. You didn't mention Alex was going to be here tonight."

Placing his arm across her chair, Aiden twirls a strand of her hair with his finger. "I don't see why we can't stay for a bit. The band sounds pretty good." He tilts his head with a shrug. "I wouldn't mind staying for a drink or two." He leans his head against hers, letting his lips lightly brush against her ear. "Look, you're mine now. This guy should know that. I won't tolerate anyone making you uncomfortable."

"You know what, you're right. I could use a drink. How about something strong," she says, winking as he gets up to leave for the bar.

With a curt nod, he kisses the top of her head. "You got it. A couple of strong drinks coming right up."

As soon as Aiden leaves the table, Emma leans over with big eyes. "Okay, what-the-fuck? You have to tell me what I've missed before he gets back to this table. Do you want to explain how the hell you left for a job interview this morning, then show up lip-locked with the CEO of the damn corporation?"

Rebecca's mouth hangs slightly open as she shakes her head, trying to think of what to say. Then, throwing her hands out, she shrugs. "It's just like Aiden said. We spent our day together, and I really like him. He's not the arrogant tight-ass I thought he was."
That statement really isn't a lie. I just left out the part about the contract.

From the smile on Aiden's face, he has obviously caught the tail end of their conversation as he returns to the table with a tray of drinks. True to his word, he's not about to let anyone make Rebecca uncomfortable. Nestling a shooter into Rebecca's hand, he raises his glass to hers, bringing Emma's interrogation to an abrupt end. "I'd like to propose a toast. To us, new beginnings and amazing discoveries," he says, clinking his glass with hers.

No sooner do they set their glasses down, and Alex's voice

echoes over the noise of the crowd. "Ladies and gentlemen, we're going to take a short break while we turn the stage over to DJ Slim for the next 20 minutes. We'll be back shortly. So don't go anywhere."

The DJ's voice ricochets through the room as a popular dance beat fills the air, and the band makes their way to the table. Alex glides up behind Rebecca with a big smile and open arms. "Hey, Becca! God, I've missed you. Come here and give me a hug."

Her eyes briefly meet Aiden's before she turns to look up at Alex with a forced smile. "Alex, How've you been?" She stands, giving him a quick hug, then swings around, gesturing to Aiden. "This is my—"

Before she can finish, Alex interrupts. "Aiden Collins – Collins Enterprises, right? Yeah, I know who he is. Wow, it's nice to meet you." Shaking Aiden's hand, he looks back at Rebecca with a stoic mask in place. "I guess I should have called more, huh. I'm really sorry, Becca. For what it's worth, I thought about you every day." He places a chaste kiss on her cheek, stepping back with a forced smile. "Well, I hope you two are sticking around. When we go back up, we'll be performing a new single I wrote. It won't officially be released for a couple more days, but I'd really like you to hear it." He places his hand on Aiden's shoulder. "You're a lucky son of a bitch, Collins. Becca's a great girl."

Pulling Rebecca into his side, Aiden kisses the top of her head. "That's not something I need to be told. I recognized that the first day I met her."

"Right. Only a fool would miss that." With a crooked

smile, Alex raises his hand to Rebecca and winks. "I guess I'll catch you guys later. Enjoy the show." Hanging his head, he walks over to take his seat at the opposite end of the table.

"He never bothered to call at all. Did he?" Resting her chin on her hand, she closes her eyes to avoid his gaze. "Nope."

Running his hand over the side of his face, Aiden shakes his head. "He's a damn fool, Rebecca." He slides a shot glass into her hand. "Here, it's the something strong you asked for," he says with a smirk.

Without hesitation, she shoots it back, blowing out the burn. There's a fire burning its way to her stomach, but since it's almost masking the sting of seeing Alex, she wants more. Noticing a second shot glass next to Aiden's arm, she motions to it. "Do you mind?"

He shakes his head, sliding it over, and watches as she slams it back as if it were cough syrup. "Better now?"

Sucking air in past her teeth, she blows it back out through O-shaped lips and nods. "Yep, the burn seems to override the sting just fine."

"Good," Aiden chuckles. "Here, try this. It's gin and tonic. I figured you might need something refreshing after the something strong."

Taking a sip, she swirls the liquid around in her mouth for a brief moment. "Hmm, you're right. It is refreshing." Gulping it back, she sets the empty glass on the table and takes his hand. "Can you dance, old man?"

Can I dance?
Raising his brow, Aiden runs his hand over his chin. *She has no idea dancing was how Max and I paid my way through college.* "I might know a move or two," he says, letting her lead him onto the dance floor.

As he starts to move around her to Please Me by Cardi B and Bruno Mars, Rebecca stands back with her mouth open. Never in her wildest dreams did she imagine he was hiding those moves under his suit and tie. She's completely blown away when the music fades to Call out My Name by The Weeknd, and Aiden pulls her back against his chest. His lips lightly brushing over her neck as he grinds the swell of his arousal into her backside. Her body begins to relax, forming to his as she fluidly responds to his every move. Then suddenly, she stops, and Aiden follows her gaze to the table.
To Alex.

Aiden's voice is soft as he leans his head against her cheek, but it carries much wisdom. "Even if I'm not your future, Rebecca, you deserve better than someone like that." He grasps her hips, turning her to face him and his lips press against hers—a passionate exchange that's just enough to make her refocus.

The microphone squeals as the music fades, and Alex's voice echoes through the speakers once again. "Thanks for sticking around. I have a new song I wrote for the love of my life." He chuckles softly, seemingly to himself, as he shakes his head. "Well, let's just say it's been a long road of could-haves and should-haves. Some may even say it's too little too late, but uh, here it is anyway. It's called Becca."

Rebecca sinks into Aiden's big chest as he wraps his arms around her waist and holds her close. "I'm guessing that's you."

She stares up at the stage. "Yeah, well, even if it is, I agree – it's too little too late."

Swaying her in his arms, Aiden lays his head against hers as they watch Alex close his eyes and belt out a beautiful ballad. When he opens his eyes halfway through the song, he peers down at Rebecca and attempts a smile. Aiden tightens his arms around her and leans in close to her ear. "Rebecca, I won't interfere with real love. If you feel—"

Rebecca spins around in his arms, shaking her head. "No. It's not real love – it never was." She leans in, pressing a soft kiss to his lips. "Besides, you can't let me go now - we have a contract."

"Ah, you're right. We do," Aiden beams.

As the song ends, they make their way to the table, and Rebecca sits on Aiden's lap - her fingers lightly toying with the back of his hair. She looks up at the stage as Alex announces last call at the bar and realizes it's finally over between them. Well, that, and that she doesn't need anymore to drink. Between the tequila shooters and the gin and tonic, she's had her limit.

When Alex walks over and places his hand on her shoulder, the tiger that punched Aiden in the jaw earlier threatens to re-emerge. "Hey, Becca. Can I talk to you alone for a minute?"

Lifting her head from Aiden's neck, she peers up through

gin goggles, trying to focus on his face. With no luck, she waves him off, nearly sliding off Aiden's lap with a giggle. "Alex, I don't have anything to say to you. The song was lovely, but it must be for some other Becca you've been traipsing around with. 'Cause if you wrote it for me, you were right – it's too little, too late." Wrapping her arms around Aiden's shoulders, she snuggles in against his chest. "You should take me home. I've punched my share of people for one day."

Aiden smirks, lifting her into his arms. "Well, Alex, that doesn't sound like it would be a very friendly conversation." He glances down to Rebecca, cradled against him. "You should consider yourself lucky. At least she gave you a warning." Before Alex can walk away, Aiden decides he'll pour a little salt on the wound for Rebecca's sake. "Oh hey, just one more thing. Could you let Emma know she'll be spending the night at my place?" The corner of his mouth tugs into a smile as he shrugs. "I don't want her to worry."

"Yeah, sure. I'll let her know," Alex says, sounding almost disconnected.

Tightening her grip around Aiden's neck, Rebecca snuggles in a little closer as he carries her out the door. "Thanks. I don't think I could've made it through tonight without you."

He sits her into the passenger seat and buckles her in, but she won't let go of his neck. "Don't let me go, Aiden. You smell so bloody good."

A growl rumbles deep in his throat as he unravels her arms from her neck. "Rebecca, trust me. Nothing would make me happier than to hold you, but we need to go home, and in order to do that, I need to drive." Stepping back, he takes another look at the young lady curled up in his front seat and mumbles under his breath. "Honestly, I'd like to do a lot more than hold you, but luckily for you, I'm more of a gentleman than that." He carefully closes her door and walks around to the driver's side.

Starting the engine, he leans his head against the headrest and exhales. He still can't believe he's finally taking her home with him. Of course, he didn't expect her to be passed out drunk on their first night together, but it has been a day full of unexpected events.

They're not too far from his place when Rebecca starts flailing about. Her seatbelt unclips, and she begins to groan, pulling at her dress. "What's wrong, Rebecca? What are you doing?"

"My god, Aiden! It's so damn hot in here."

Of course, his car has air-conditioning, but why deny himself the guilty pleasure of watching her struggle out of that dress. He keeps glancing over, watching the dress inch further up her body every time he turns his head. When she finally wins the battle, she tosses it into the backseat with a triumphant smile. His current view is now a beautiful young lady in nothing more than a pair of skimpy panties and those sexy stilettos, and he's struggling to keep his eye on the road.

He takes a deep breath, shifting to give his growing erection some space. "You know, you could have asked me to turn on the air conditioning."

Rebecca rolls her head to face him, her mouth agape.

"How am I supposed to know you have air conditioning? You should have told me."

"Yes. I suppose I could have," Aiden shrugs, scanning her bared flesh.

Throwing her arms out, she slaps them down, smoothing her hands over the seat. "Well, it's too late now. Anyway, I like the feel of leather against my skin."

Raising his brow, Aiden smiles as he pulls into his driveway and parks in front of the house. "Then sadly, I hate to announce we're home."

She springs forward and gazes out the window at the huge house she could only dream of living in. "Are you shitting me? This is where you live?"

"Yes. I thought you did your homework, Miss D'Angelo," he says, stepping out with a sly smile. When he opens her door, she's still gazing up as her foot hits the ground. "Would you like help putting your dress on, or should I carry you in as you are?"

The corner of her mouth lifts. "I'm sure I can walk, but if you insist on carrying me" – she opens her arms – "by all means. There's not much sense in struggling with the dress. I mean, you've already seen most of me, and your contract promises intimate encounters, right?"

Aiden laughs. "I'm certainly not going to argue about carrying you in as you are, but there won't be any intimate encounters tonight, Rebecca."

As he bends down, she wraps her arms around his neck. "Hey Aiden, I think I should tell you something, especially since we'll be living together for the next few weeks," her words a bit of a slur. "I really hate clothes. I have since I was a child."

His smile broadens. "Honestly, Rebecca, I can't say that's a disappointment." Then, sliding his hand under her legs, he pulls her pliant body against him and lifts her into his arms. "Let's get you into bed. We can discuss your likes and dislikes tomorrow when the alcohol wears off."

Kicking the car door shut, he turns toward the house with Rebecca giggling in his arms. She twists her fingers through the top of his hair playfully, then groans, "Aww, come on, Aiden. I'm not ready for bed yet. Let's discuss those intimate encounters, shall we?"

Rolling her tighter against him to punch in his security code for the door, he looks down at her and grins. "Oh, I think you are ready for bed. We can discuss everything tomorrow."

"Pfft. I might have signed your contract, Mr. Collins, but I didn't see a clause that said anything about my bedtime." Her eyes light up as they enter the house, and she begins to wiggle in his arms. "Wow, this place is amazing. Do you have a pool?" Her hand flies to her forehead as she laughs. "God, what am I saying? Of course, you have a pool," she says, kicking off her shoes as she cranes her head to look around.

"Mmhmm, you're right, I do." She twists so quickly he's unable to catch her before she launches herself from his arms.

Barely landing on her feet, Aiden catches her by the waist moments before she topples over. "Whoa! You are quick, Mr. Collins," she says, waving her finger with a chuckle.

"Lead me to your pool. Let's go skinny dipping!"

Skinny dipping? Christ, I'll never be able to control myself with her naked in the pool. It seems a fair warning is in order, but if she persists, then all bets are off. I am just a man, after all, and watching her strip down in my car to those damn stilettos hasn't helped the raging hard-on I've been fighting all night.

"Rebecca, I need to warn you. I'm not sure I'd be able to keep my hands off you if we go skinny dipping. In fact, I know I won't. I really think we should get you a t-shirt and call it a night."

Standing in front of him in nothing but her panties, she runs her hands down his chest and sticks out her bottom lip. "Aw, don't be a party-pooper, Aiden. I don't want a t-shirt. I want you to get undressed and take me to the pool. Your contract promised intimate moments. Why can't they start tonight?"

Done!
I tried to be the good guy. Yet, she continues to tempt me.
Now, I'll gladly be taking what's mine!

A low groan comes from his chest as he strips off his shirt and tosses it to the floor. Aiden is not a stupid man. He knows Rebecca's shyness has been lost somewhere in a bottle of gin, but the way she's actively eye-fucking him as he unbuttons his jeans – could make any man cave. He lets his eyes rove the length of her body, stopping briefly to admire the tiny red 'V' at the top of her thighs before his jeans hit the floor. Then, stepping over the material, he tucks his finger into the waistband of her panties and peers into her eyes. "Are you sure you want to go to the pool? I have a king-size bed upstairs."

A flush works over her body, and he would put money on the fact it's not from embarrassment. Nope, that's pure lustful need seeping through her flesh. "Mmhmm, I'm sure," she says, biting her bottom lip as she takes his hand. "The pool, please." Leading her out to the patio, he flicks the switch, and her eyes come to life with the lights. "Sweet!"

Smiling at her amazement, Aiden grabs two water bottles, sets them down on the edge, then gestures toward the stairs. "After you, pretty lady."

Without hesitation, she takes a few steps back and runs, leaping into the pool. When she breaches the surface, she tosses her panties at Aiden's feet with a giggle. "Okay, it's your turn," she calls out with a grin.

He's not about to analyze the many sides of Rebecca right now, especially when the vivid images of what will happen once he gets into that water begin to dance through his mind. Instead, he swallows and drops his boxers to the deck. Diving in, he swims up behind her, slinks his arms around her waist and pulls her tight to his chest. His tongue runs along the side of her neck as he presses his erection against her bottom. "Jesus, Rebecca, I could easily lose myself to a woman like you."

She turns in his arms, placing her hands on his face with a slight smile. "Let's not tease, Mr. Collins. We both know this is only for 30 days." She runs the back of her finger over the short beard she's been admiring all day. "Hmm, it really is as soft as it looks," she says, leaning in to kiss him.

Smiling, Aiden leans forward, guiding her back toward the wall. "You have me naked in my pool, and you're suddenly interested in my beard?" Rebecca's giggle ceases as her back meets the wall of the pool. Her eyes jump from his intense stare to his mouth as he leans forward, pressing his lips to hers. When their tongues meet, she grips his shoulders and swings her legs around his waist – an invitation by Aiden's standards. He grabs the back of her thighs, gently squeezing as he pulls her closer.

Anything Rebecca thought she knew about sex, she's about to find out she hadn't a clue. She hasn't been with a real man before. The only experience she's had with sex, beyond her vibrator, was with Alex when they were sixteen. Her head falls back, and Aiden slides his hand under her bottom, his fingers reaching for her most delicate part. His lips press against the crease of her neck as he growls, "Jesus, Rebecca. You have no idea how badly I want to be inside you right now."

Her centre twitches as it hits his flesh, sending a warm sprite through her stomach, and she arches her back, pushing her breast against his face. Hungrily sucking her nipple into his mouth, Aiden presses his finger into her opening. "Ah yes," she moans, grabbing his hair to pull him closer - her legs flexing against his back, trying to drive the new invasion deeper.

Removing his hand, Aiden lifts his head, his chest heaving as he licks the water from his lips. "Rebecca, when is the last time you had sex?"

Her eyes spring to his as her mouth drops open. "Really, Aiden? You weren't concerned about the last time I had sex when you wanted me to sign your contract."

Raising a brow, Aiden tips his head, his chest rising as he

inhales.

She's right. It wasn't something I ever questioned.

He looks into her eyes, "Look, I'm not judging you, Rebecca. It's, well, quite frankly, it's snug down there. I guess I just want to be sure that you're not still a virgin."

She glares at him. "Jesus, Aiden!" Dropping her hands from his shoulders, she slaps the surface of the water. "I'm not a damn virgin. I mean, sure, maybe it's been a while. I was sixteen when Alex and I had sex, but we agreed we would wait until our wedding night after that. Things just didn't work out between us." She shakes her head, chewing on her bottom lip. "What does that even matter?"

Taking a deep breath, he leans his forehead against her shoulder.

Holy fuck! Could I really be this blessed?

"You're right," he says, lifting his head to look into her eyes. "I guess it doesn't matter. I just want you to enjoy this as much as I know I will."

With a devil-may-care smile, she shrugs. "I was feeling great until you stopped." She wraps her arms around his neck and pulls him closer. Nipping at his bottom lip, she loosens her thighs around his waist and lets her bottom drop till the head of his member is resting against her opening. Her insides flip, releasing a wave of nervous butterflies and her breath catches. Aiden's eyes meet hers as she begins to slowly roll her hips, trying to manoeuvre him deeper into her entrance.

He grasps her hips. "Rebecca, let me take you inside. This can be so much more enjoyable on a comfortable bed. The last thing I want is for this to be a bad experience."

She narrows her eyes, tightening her legs around his waist. "No, Aiden, you wanted this! And trust me, at this moment, there's nothing that I want or need more. So let's just fucking do it!"

Her brazen words have him throbbing at her opening, and he's not about to argue. Instead, he grabs her bottom, peers into her eyes and repositions himself. "All right, just be sure to let me know if it's too much."

He gently begins to slide upward, inch by agonizing inch, when Rebecca digs her hands into his hair. "Don't go slow!"

Done!

Aiden's hands slide to her thighs, spreading her open, and with one quick thrust, he groans, feeling her warm body accept him.

She gasps, her fingernails digging deep into his shoulders while her muscles protest around him. "Shit!"

He stills, brushing a strand of hair from her face while he allows her body time to adjust. "Are you okay? Should we stop?"

Biting her lip, Rebecca shakes her head. "Are you kidding? My body is screaming for release." Her voice rising an octave as her eyes widen. "I need to cum. Just stop stalling and do it, or I'll do it my damn self!"

Aiden smiles, loving how she's been holding this wild side so close to her chest. He backs out then pushes in, gaining a little more depth with each stroke. "I promise I'll get you there, baby, but you need to loosen your muscles a little."

Drawing her bottom lip between her teeth, she feels his fingers slowly working their way toward her sweet spot. "Oh my god, Aiden," she gasps, her back curling with a moan.

He thrusts into her as she relaxes her muscles. "That's it, baby, open up for me."

Her stomach tightens with the wave of nervous excitement rushing through her, and she pulls him closer. Her legs flexing against his back as she rises and lowers herself along his shaft – his name leaving her lips as if he were the new god. "Oh, Aiden!"

As her orgasm consumes her, each throbbing pulse drags him deeper into her warmth. He can't pull his eyes from her face. Watching her lose herself on him is so erotic – so intense.

Her breath catches, coming out in short bursts as her thighs begin to tremble. Thankful that she's found her release, Aiden grabs her bottom, immersing himself in her pleasure. He thrusts forward, surrounding himself with her contracting muscles – her warm, soft flesh wrapping him like a pulsating vice.

He thrusts once.
Twice.
He tightens his grip, pulling her against him and squeezes his eyes shut. "Ahhh – yes!"

Rebecca can feel his heart racing under her hands as he exhales through pursed lips repeatedly next to her ear, trying to bring himself back to the present. Finally, he drops his head to her shoulder and releases a long breath.

"Jesus, that was amazing. I haven't been that wound since I was a teenager."

Lightly kissing her cheek, he shifts out of her hold and slowly pulls away. "I still say it would have been better for you if you had let me take you up to bed," he says, wrapping a towel around his waist as he hands her a bottle of water.

"Would it have made that much of a difference?" she asks, opening her water to take a drink.

Aiden shrugs. "It probably would have been a little more pleasant for you in a more controlled environment."

She accepts his extended hand allowing him to help her out of the pool and settles in on his lap.
"I think you controlled our environment perfectly."

"Yes, well, I'm glad you approve since your demanding little self gave me no choice of our environment," he says with a wink as he drapes a towel across her hips and kisses her cheek. "So, tell me the truth. Is that why you panicked and agreed to the contract when you realized Alex was at the bar tonight? You didn't know how else to say no to your first love?"

"Mmhmm. Well, no. I don't know. It's not just that." She looks down at her lap, trying to hide the blush she can feel surfacing on her cheeks. "Truthfully, I couldn't bear the humiliation of him knowing I hadn't moved on yet. I mean, I guess I have – mentally. I don't think I want him anymore. I just haven't attempted to date anyone since he left." Her gaze moves back to his. "And obviously, he's been with a ton of women since he left. Or really, not only since he left. Alex has always had a problem with being faithful. I've caught him cheating too many times to count, but somehow, he's always had a way of convincing me it wasn't his fault or that it was all in my mind. You know, jealousy. I mean, even when the evidence was glaring right at me, I still caved and gave him the benefit of the doubt" – she shrugs – "I loved him."

Realizing she used him to get back at her ex-boyfriend, he forces a smile and gives her a knowing nod.

Fair enough. Whatever the reason, it just cost her the next 30 days at my whim.

With this new understanding, he lifts her into his arms and kisses her cheek. "Well, I'd say his loss is my gain. I'm certainly not going to dwell on it, and I hope you've truly let him go – for your sake. Why don't we get some sleep? We need to go find you a car in the morning, and it's almost 4 am."

"I don't expect you to buy me a car, Aiden."

"Hush, we're getting you a car. It's the least I can do since I had yours towed," he says, lowering her onto the bed. As he hovers above her, he brushes her hair from her face. "To be clear, Rebecca. With or without a contract, you're not some conquest as you may think." Laying a soft kiss on her cheek, he climbs into bed and pulls her against his chest. "Sweet dreams."

Thoroughly sated, she tucks the sheet against her chin and closes her eyes. "Thanks, Aiden. I needed to hear that."

Chapter 4 – Max

The following morning they're awakened by heavy banging on the bedroom door accompanied by a roaring voice. "Come on, Aiden. Get your punk ass up! I know you're in there. Your car's in the driveway, and I just saw the panties of last night's victim out by the pool."

Releasing a groan next to Rebecca's ear, Aiden pulls her tighter to his chest. "Just ignore him. That's the sound of an idiot – one that's not supposed to be here. With any luck, he'll go away." Luckily, semi-conscious Rebecca realizes she's naked and reaches for the sheet just as the door bursts open. Aiden quickly flies up, ensuring she's covered and gives their intruder a mouthful. "What-the-fuck, Max?! You can't just barge in here. Get out!"

Laughing, Max covers his mouth with his fist. "Oh shit, sorry, man." He throws his hand up in defence. "How was I supposed to know you'd have a chick in here? When did you start letting chicks spend the night?"

Rebecca takes a second glance at Aiden's double standing by the door. She covers her reddening face with the sheet while trying to melt into Aiden's chest, her mind spinning off in confusion.

A twin! He has a freaking twin? Why didn't I know about this? I've researched this man and his company inside and out—or I thought I did.

Keeping a protective arm tightly across her chest, Aiden lifts himself onto his elbow to finish dishing it to Max. "Since I've started dating someone! Now watch your mouth, and remember this is my fucking house." He cranes his neck to look at the alarm clock beside the bed and glares back up at him. "What are you doing here, anyway? Do you realize it's eight o'clock in the morning? Besides, I thought you were going to be in Seattle for another month."

"Yeah, until I called the office and Natasha said you took the next month off. Being your caring older brother, I thought I'd make sure you were okay." Max gestures to Rebecca on the bed next to him and smiles. "But now, I'm starting to understand why. Aren't you at least going to introduce us?"

"Oh, for christ's sake, knock off the older brother bullshit. It's two fucking minutes, Max!" Aiden uncovers Rebecca's face keeping his arm tight across her chest. "Rebecca, in case you haven't put the pieces together yet – I have a twin brother. No, let me rephrase that. I have an annoying loud-mouth twin brother. His name is Max."

"It's nice to meet you, Becca," Max says, leaning down with his hand extended.

Aiden smacks it away. "Fuck off, man! What are you thinking? She's not about to bare herself to you!"

"All right, all right!" Max laughs, putting his hand up in front of him. "I'll wait downstairs, but hurry up." He scans the length of Rebecca's body, shaking his head. "Damn girl, you must be someone pretty special to spend the night in the playboy's forbidden den," he says, stalking out of the room.

Dropping his elbow, Aiden gazes down at her with an awkward smile. "I'm sorry about that. He was supposed to be in Seattle."

His lips lightly graze hers, igniting some embers from the night before. "Mmm, good morning," she says, pulling him down for another kiss.

"Rebecca, I would love to spend the day in bed doing unspeakable things to you. However, now that Max knows you're here, he won't let up until we go downstairs. Besides, I promised we'd find you a new car today, remember?"

Sitting up, she holds the sheet tight to her chest. "There's just one small problem. I have no clothes. If I remember correctly, my dress is on the floor of your car." She fans her hand toward the door. "And according to your brother, my panties are out by the pool. I don't have any of my clothes here."

He runs his hand through his hair, smiling as he grabs his phone. "You're right. Not to worry. I'll take care of your clothing." Pressing a button on his phone, he places it to his ear and winks. "Good morning Natasha. I need you to send over a few outfits for Rebecca." He puts his hand over the phone, chucking his chin in her direction. "What size do you wear?"

"Oh, um, five?"

"Size five, you've seen her. Feel free to use your discretion." He goes quiet, listening to what's being said on the other end. "Sure, use the Gucci account. She'll need at least three outfits for today, undergarments included. Oh, and be sure to add a bathing suit. Have them rush the order, please. You can order her a full wardrobe, but I need this order right away." He pauses briefly to listen, walking toward his dresser. "Sure, I think that should be fine until Friday. Thank you." Hanging up, he smiles, tossing her one of his t-shirts. "You'll have to throw this on for now. We'll shower after breakfast. Hopefully, your clothes will be here by then."

Throwing his t-shirt over her head, she pulls herself out of bed. "I have no underwear."

With a sly grin, he slides his hand between her thighs, sweeping his thumb through her folds. "Mmm, the things I would love to do to you right now." He sucks his thumb into his mouth with a wink. "Unfortunately, we have Max waiting for us downstairs, and we have a car to find." Placing a kiss on her forehead, he pats her bottom. "Now, let's go before I take what's rightfully mine. I really have no qualms with Max's persistent banging on the bedroom door."

Rebecca's jaw suddenly becomes unhinged as she watches the cocky grin form across his face. Cupping her chin, he lifts her slack jaw and plants a hard kiss on her lips. "Oh, come now, don't look so surprised. If I recall correctly, you didn't check off any boxes before signing our contract last night. That means I have zero restrictions when it comes to your body for the next 30 days."

Rebecca is suddenly finding it difficult to swallow. She never even read the list, only the first few items. She grabs his arm and gazes up at him with pleading eyes. "Aiden, I jumped the gun on signing that contract. I never even read the list. Can't I at least go over it and make my choices now?"

His laugh sounds almost sinister as he pulls her into his chest and brushes the hair from her face. "Oh, no, baby. It doesn't work that way. Like I said last night, don't forget it can't be changed once it's signed. Besides, you're not a child, remember? You know how contracts work."

His cobalt eyes show just a touch of compassion as he strokes her hair. "Look, I'll tell you what. I know you got a little antsy because of an ex-boyfriend. So, I'm going to be generous here and go against my own policy. I'll let you look it over and check off just one definite no when we get back home."

Her brows draw together, and you'd swear she just stomped her foot. "But, Aiden, there had to be at least fifty items listed on that page!"

Taking her hand, he leads her toward the door. "Now, thanks to my generosity, you'll only have to worry about forty-nine of them," he chuckles. "Let's be honest, you're not even sure of what you like or don't like yet. Now, let's go get something to eat."

Rebecca's shoulders slump.
Mom always said my spontaneous nature would get me into a tight spot one day. I mean, I'm sure there's nothing to worry about. He was such a gentleman last night. I can see him throwing a little oral into the mix. Maybe even a vibrator. Shit, I can live with that. That sounds like it could be a lot of fun.

Max is sitting at the kitchen table with a cup of coffee when they walk in. Gesturing toward the coffee pot with his cup, he scans Rebecca from head to toe while she watches a slow sexy smile form across his face. "There's coffee in the pot, gorgeous."

Aiden pulls out a chair and puts his hand on her shoulder. "Sit. I'll bring the coffee over." His eyes cut to Max. "Don't you have somewhere else to be?"

"Nope. I solidified the office setup in Seattle. It was simple as shit." He slaps his hands together with a grin. "You can check with Natasha. That's why I thought I'd come for breakfast and see why you needed a month off." His deep blue eyes lock with Rebecca's as he smirks. "Now that I understand the need for a holiday, where's my breakfast, bro? I'm starving."

Setting the coffee on the table, Aiden makes it a point to ignore Max completely. "What would you like for breakfast, Rebecca? I can make you bacon and eggs, or how about some pancakes."

Max chuckles, leaning across the table. "Hey, Becca. Since you have all the pull with that pussy of yours, can you pick bacon and eggs, please?"

Rebecca can't help but smile. Max seems to have the ability to piss Aiden off easily.

Picking up a spoon from the table, Aiden chucks it at Max. "Shut the fuck up! Your 29 years old, not 19 anymore, Max. Have some fucking respect or leave."

Laughing, Max leans back with his hands up as if to surrender. It's not hard to tell this is a customary game. Trying to diffuse the sibling tension building around the table, Rebecca reaches for Aiden's hand and gives it a light kiss. "I can't believe you didn't tell me you had a twin – an identical one at that. I mean, damn, I'd love just to have a sibling, but a twin. That must be amazing." She gives Max a bright smile then looks over at Aiden. "You know what? Bacon and eggs really do sound great. Why don't I give you a hand?"

As she starts to stand, Aiden rests his hand on her shoulder. "Oh no, I'm not having Max ogle you while you make his damn breakfast. You sit and enjoy your coffee. Just let me know if he gets out of line."

So, Max, huh? I like Max. He's quite interesting. Definitely no mistaking these two are twins, but there are some visual differences. Max's hair is a bit longer, and his beard isn't as well kept as Aiden's. Oh, and one thing is very apparent, they have entirely different personalities. Max is kind of rough around the edges. In fact, he's actually quite boisterous now that I think about it – not refined like Aiden. I highly doubt Max even owns a suit. He seems right at home in those jeans and that t-shirt. I mean, he's the kind of guy that openly says things like pussy without even batting an eye. Aiden is definitely more of a gentleman. He doesn't talk like Max, and he certainly wouldn't openly ogle a woman like Max just did this morning. I'd have to say, Max is the hot dirty side of the Collins brothers.

Shaking Rebecca from her mental comparison, Max slips a card into the palm of her hand and looks at her matter-of-factly. "Listen, Princess. If Aiden ever mistreats you in any way, you call me. I'll gladly come get you, no questions asked." She bursts out laughing as a roll of paper towel flies across the kitchen, hitting Max in the head.

Aiden's deep voice rumbles from the other side of the kitchen island. "Max! I said, knock it off!"

He leans down and picks up the roll of paper towel, chuckling as he sets it up on the table and swipes the bangs back from his face. It's not hard to tell Max gets a thrill out of pissing off his brother. "So, tell me. Where did Aiden find a pretty little thing like you anyway?"

She's about to answer when Aiden appears at her side with plates and utensils. "This is the little beauty I told you about before you left for Seattle. Remember, the young lady that spilled her latte on me at the office?" He smiles at his brother, and suddenly it looks like something in Max's demeanour changes.

Leaning back in his chair, Max rubs his chin with a mischievous smile. "Well shit, so you're the infamous latte beauty."

With a hint of embarrassment, Rebecca nods. "Yeah, I guess I am."

Oh my god! How many people has he told about my ruining his suit?

Aiden places a bowl of scrambled eggs and a plate of bacon on the table and takes his seat. Taking Rebecca's hand, he kisses it lightly. "Her name is Rebecca. Use it." He waves his hand in the air as if to close the conversation. "Now, forget about the damn latte incident and eat. Rebecca and I are going out after breakfast." As Aiden reaches for his fork, the doorbell chimes. He takes a deep breath and tosses his napkin onto the table. Looking over at Max, he gives him a taunting smile and places his hand on Rebecca's shoulder. "Ahh, that must be your clothes. I'll be right back."

Taking a bite of her bacon, Rebecca feels Max staring and finds the urge to break the silence overwhelming. "So, um, you and Aiden are partners then? I mean, you both run Collins Enterprises."

Nodding, he shovels a forkful of eggs into his mouth, chews once and swallows.

Damn, this boy is a beast.

"Yeah, I guess you could say that." He sits back for a minute, studying her before he goes back to eating his breakfast. "Nah, you know what? It's Aiden's company. Natasha will call me in the odd time if Aiden's away, but that's very rare." He meets Rebecca's eyes. "This trip to Seattle was a first and likely the last business trip for me." Smiling, he shrugs. "Anyway, he's in control. Everything goes through him when it comes to the business."

Aiden sits back down to join them and picks up his fork. "What business?"

Max leans back and takes a sip of his coffee. "Oh, she asked if we were partners." Setting his cup down, he chucks his chin. "Where are you two off to today anyway?"

"Well, I owe Rebecca a car. I accidentally had hers towed and promised to replace it."

Rebecca can feel herself stiffen as she glares over at him. "That's a lie, Aiden! It wasn't accidental at all." Suddenly she begins to think of where she'd be right now if not for him having it towed. She knows all too well she would have fallen for Alex's nonsense like she always does. She would have regrettably woken up beside him this morning.

Her face softens as Aiden takes her hand with a smirk. "Right. Well, tomato tomáhto Rebecca. I still owe you a car."

She shrugs. "I actually don't mind your chauffeur services. I have nowhere to go that you won't be accompanying me for the next month anyway. So there's really no rush. Besides, I'm not even mad anymore," she says, looking at Aiden out of the corner of her eye as she takes a sip of her coffee.

Max holds up his coffee mug, chucking his chin at Aiden. "Shit, bro, you must have been top of your game last night. Personally, I'd cut your sac off if you had my car towed."

Aiden smirks as he scans Rebecca's face. He knows all too well her 30-day reference was about the contract. Thankfully, Max didn't catch it. Besides, as crazy as it sounds, he can already picture a future with this girl. "Yeah, well, I'm not playing a game, Bro."

Rebecca clears her throat and takes a drink of her coffee. She doesn't want this conversation to get too deep, especially with Max as a participant. "Okay then, what kind of car are we getting? The same type as the one I had?"

Aiden looks up from under his brow. "I'm afraid they don't make cars like that anymore, Rebecca."

"Are you going to Island Auto downtown? I heard they have the new E400 convertibles in stock. She'd look hot behind the wheel of one of those," Max says, giving her a wink. "Trust me. You want this car." Rebecca opens her mouth as if she's about to say something when Max raises his hands defensively. "I'm just trying to help you out here, babe. Think big. He can afford it."

Did he just call me babe?
"Well, I'm sure we'll be able to get something close to what I had." She stands, laying her hand on Aiden's shoulders. "I'm going to go for a quick shower now that my clothes are here." Her eyes shift to Max, giving him a bright smile. "It was great to meet you, Max."

Hoping Max will have left by the time she gets back downstairs, she heads up to Aiden's room. She can't believe the size of the ensuite – it's enormous. There's a bricked glass wall divider that separates the toilet from the bathing area, and just past that is a double soaker tub and shower with a cascading water wall between the two. "This man has way too much money," she says, shaking her head.

Opening the shower door, she turns the dial, sets the temperature, then presses the button to turn on the water. Stripping off Aiden's t-shirt, she climbs into the massive glass stall. Squirting some shampoo into her palm, she begins to lather it into her hair when she hears the bathroom door click. Aiden's deep voice echoes above the spray of the shower only moments before his fingers dance across her ribs. "Hey, I thought you would have waited for me."

"I'm sorry. I knew you wanted to go, and you have your brother here." She finishes rinsing her hair and turns to face him. "You should have told me you were planning on joining me. I would have waited."

He takes the soap from the dish, rolling it in his hand to build a good lather. "Max is going to come with us to the dealership." Returning the soap, he reaches down and taps her inner thigh. "Spread your legs. Max really knows his cars, and I think he could be an asset in finding the right vehicle for you. Go ahead and rinse," he says, running his hand under the water.

She lifts her leg, resting her foot on the ledge to rinse as Aiden steps forward to stand between her thighs. His once flaccid member is now firm and pointing toward its desire. Gently taking her jaw in his hand, he licks a droplet of water from her lip before running the back of his fingers over her breast. He smiles at the slight 'ah' she makes and grabs her leg, preventing her from putting it down. "Nuh-uh, don't move. Stay exactly like that."

Nervous anticipation fills her stomach as she watches him kiss his way down the front of her to kneel at her feet. "Now? Here? But I thought you said we didn't have time this morning."

He looks up, licking just below her belly button and winks. "Yes, well, Max was banging at the door then."

Sliding his fingers through her folds, she lets out a light 'ah,' pressing her hips toward him as he slips his finger inside. Continuing to kiss his way down from her navel, he stops at the top of her slit, tapping her thigh as he shrugs his shoulder. "Set your foot up here," he says, resting back on his heels.

Rebecca lifts her leg, placing her foot on his shoulder, and he slides between her thighs, cupping her bottom in his hand. With a long leisurely lap of his tongue, he closes his mouth over her mound and sucks her in. Waves of excitement ripple through her every limb. Her hand flies to the back of his head as she struggles to remain standing, her toes curling into the tiles as her thighs start to shake. Her moans ring out around them as he withdraws his finger and backs away.

Rebecca's body is still pulsating when Aiden stands, licking his lips with a grin. "I don't think you'll need to worry about that item any longer." He teases her nipple between his thumb and forefinger while using his other hand to settle himself against her entrance. "See, Rebecca, it's all about discovery."

She's still trying to catch her breath when her heavy lids finally allow her to focus on him. "Aiden, what about —" But before she can finish what she's about to say, his mouth covers hers, swallowing her words as his tongue sweeps away any rational thoughts. With one hand on her lower back and the other in her hair, he thrusts into her.

"Jesus, Rebecca, you feel so fucking good." His hands slide down her back to cradle her bottom. "Wrap your legs around me, baby."

She grips his shoulders and anchors her legs around his waist. With his hands under her bottom, he guides her along his shaft, reviving the waves of pleasure that made her see stars. Her muscles once again begin to tense. "Oh my god, Aiden — don't stop!" As her feral moans echo through the bathroom, not a soul within 100 yards could deny that he owns her body. Her back hits the cool tiles of the shower as his thrusts become deeper, more determined, inching her up with every powerful pump.

As he drives himself into her, he gazes down at the vision

before him – this young woman that's so easily stealing his heart. Her flesh is flushed from her recent release, and her eyes closed with her lips slightly parted, wet strands of her long blond hair hugging her breasts as they bounce with each thrust. "Shit, baby, if you could only see just how fucking hot you look right now."

Finally, with his eyes fixed on the beauty before him, he bends his knees, driving forth with one last push. Her inner walls scream with a painful pleasure she will now always crave as they relentlessly spasm around him.

"Fuck, Rebecca, having you could become an addiction," he pants, dropping his head into the crevice of her neck.

God, I hope so because you're quickly becoming mine.
As the orgasmic haze clears, embarrassment starts to set in. "Shit! You said your brother is still here waiting for us?"

He shrugs, wrapping a towel around his waist, drawing Rebecca's eyes to the impressive impression of his semi-hard manhood as he turns to face her. "I assure you Max is not naïve enough to think I was just coming up to wash your back." As his gaze falls to the pair of white short-shorts Natasha had sent over, he raises his brow and twirls his finger in a circle. "Wow. Turn around so I can see those."

Narrowing her eyes, she twists her lips and looks over her shoulder in the mirror at her bottom. She'll admit, she usually wears her shorts a bit longer, but they don't seem too extreme. Sticking her butt out, she wiggles it with a giggle before turning back to face him. "What's the problem? Do they meet your approval," she asks, pulling on the red tank top.

His hand runs across his forehead as Aiden takes a deep breath and shakes his head. "God damn it! I'm going to kill Max before this day is over. I can see it now."

Laughing, Rebecca grabs his hand. "Oh, I'm sure Max isn't that bad."

"Right," Aiden says, kissing the tip of her nose. "Well, let's go get this over with so we can lose him."

They find Max waiting in the living room watching TV. He turns around with a wide shit-eating grin. "Hey, I hope you don't mind. I had to turn on the TV to drown out the moaning. You really should consider investing in sound-proofing this place, Aiden." Heat instantly rushes to Rebecca's cheeks. She tries to divert her gaze, but it's too late. Max's eyes meet hers, and he smiles, licking his lips with a wink. "You good now, princess?"

Shit! Is it too much to ask for lightning to strike me down right now?
Rebecca slowly tries to slide in behind Aiden to hide from Max's taunting, but he pulls her against his side with a smile. "Jesus, shut up, Max. You're embarrassing her."

Max puts his hands up in surrender. "Becca, I'm sorry. I just joke around a lot. Do you forgive me?"

He extends his hand with an exaggerated pout. As she accepts his hand, he kisses her fingers, peering up with a smile. "But seriously, that was the hottest fucking orgasm I've heard out of a woman to date! I'm gonna be walking around with a chub all day, just thinking about it."

Rebecca's mouth drops open as she retrieves her hand to

cover her eyes.

Okay. It's official. I have never been so embarrassed in my life.

"Jesus, Max," Aiden says, swatting him in the back of the head. "Fucking knock it off!" Shaking his head, he pulls her back from Max. "Just ignore him. He apparently needs to get laid."

Max grunts heading for the door. "Absolutely, I'm obviously in need now. If you ask me, Aiden has his priorities in his ass, princess. I'd just order you a car offline and let you drive me all fucking day." He grabs his groin and smiles with a snap of his head. "Mmm!"

Bounding forward, Aiden moves so fast, swiping Max's legs out from under him that Max has no time to react. He lands with a loud thud on the floor, looking a little stunned. "What-the-fuck, Aiden?!"

"I said, shut the fuck up, Max!"

He takes Rebecca's hand, leading her toward the door. As they pass Max, Aiden glances at him with a sideways grin. "You coming or what?"

Embarrassment gone with Max's fall, Rebecca laughs. *I think I need to remember that the banter between these two really isn't about me. I just happen to be the centrepiece at the moment. It's not hard to tell that these two have been at this for years – likely since birth.*

Gaining his feet, Max straightens himself and smiles. "Fuck yeah, how else can I watch that sweet ass all day?"

Aiden stops, his eyes narrowing as Max throws his hands up. "All right, all right, I'm done."

Chapter 5 – The Car

When they arrive at the dealership, Max hops out of his Hummer and jogs over to Rebecca. Placing his hands on her shoulders, he leans his forehead against hers. "Okay, now, don't forget what I said. Ask him to see the new E400, and tell him you want that baby fully loaded." He chucks his chin at Aiden. "Let the lady ask for the car."

Rebecca peers back at the brothers for confidence as the salesman approaches and straightens her shoulders. "Hi, I'd like to see the new Mercedes E400, please."

Max quickly chimes out behind her, "And make sure that baby is fully loaded. If the lady likes it, we'll be taking it with us today."

A sly grin works across the salesman's face as he scans Rebecca from head to toe. When his gaze focuses on Aiden and Max standing not far behind her, he nods. "Ye-Yes, ma'am. Would you prefer to test drive the convertible or the hardtop," he asks, allowing his sly grin to return.

Max narrows his eyes as he steps up beside her and folds his arms. "I'm not sure we caught your name. Did you give it?"

"I believe I had introduced myself to the lady, Sir. I'm Lance," he says, extending his hand.

Looking down at his extended hand, Max sneers. "Okay, Lance," he says, emphasizing his name. "Why don't you go get her an E400 convertible" – Max peers over at Rebecca and smiles – "let's say in red. Oh, and we'll be coming along for the test drive. So make sure it's a 4-seater, and be sure you wipe that stupid fucking grin off your face before you get back."

Lance's smile disappears with a slow nod. "Of course, Sir. My apologies. I'll be right back."

Laughing, Aiden tucks Rebecca into his side. "Jesus, Max, chill. You're gonna make the poor guy piss his pants."

Max shrugs, settling his bottom against one of the new vehicles parked along the edge of the lot. "Let the little fucker squirm. That guy's a weasel. He was nothing short of licking his lips when he eyed Becca."

Aiden scans the length of Rebecca's body, kissing his teeth with a tilt of his head. "She's hot. Of course, he's gonna check her out. As long as he doesn't try to touch her, he can live." He draws his brows together, pointing his finger at Max. "That goes for you too. We're not kids anymore. You can look, but don't touch."

Max pushes himself off the car with a smirk. "Aw, come on now. That's not very brotherly, Aiden. Remember how Nan and Pop always taught us that sharing is caring?"

Rebecca puts her hands up, pointing to herself. "Uh, hey guys! Do you mind? I'm right here."

The sound of gravel crunching under tires alerts them to the arrival of a shiny red convertible, and Rebecca can't believe her eyes. It's freaking gorgeous! It doesn't compare to her old blue Mazda in the slightest. "Holy shit!" She grabs hold of Aiden's arm and stares at the beautiful piece of machinery in front of them. "You're not seriously considering buying this car. Are you, Aiden?"

Leading her to the driver's side, he opens the door and motions for her to get in. "I don't know. That all depends on if you like the way it handles or not. You wouldn't buy a car without test driving it, now would you," he says with a wink.

"Oh, that's very funny, Mr. Collins," she says, sliding into the driver's seat.

Max slaps his hand off the side of the car and hollers as Rebecca pulls out onto Government Street. "Come on, Becca, Take this baby out onto the highway and let's see what she's got!"

Looking over at Aiden, he smiles with a shrug, and Rebecca doesn't skip a beat. She'd love to open it up. Merging onto Pat Bay Highway, she gives it some gas, and her smile grows with the speedometer.

It's smooth,
It's sleek,
It's fast, and she loves it!
She glances over at Aiden with a wide smile, and she can tell from the look on his face—
It's Sold!

Pulling off at the next exit, she turns around and heads back to the dealership. As they exit the car, Aiden takes her hand and nods at the salesman. "Well, Lance, it's your lucky day. Why don't you get the paperwork ready so we can take it with us?"

"Oh my god! Thank you!" Rebecca wraps her arms around his neck, mashing her lips into his cheek. "I never expected something so extravagant, but I absolutely love it!"

Chuckling at her reaction, Aiden kisses her. "I'm glad you like it, Rebecca."

"Like it? Are you kidding? I love it!"

Pursing his lips, Max taps his toe and holds his arms out. "Hey, what about me? I told you about the damn car. Don't I deserve a hug?"

Aiden shakes his head. "You better watch it. If you piss her off, she has a killer right hook." Rebecca pats Aiden on the chest. "No, he's right. I wouldn't have known what to ask for."

She walks into his outstretched arms, and he lifts her into the air, giving Aiden a shit-eating grin. Laughing, she places a kiss on his cheek. "Thanks for your help, Max. It's perfect!" She lets go of his neck and starts to turn away when he scoops her up into his arms whirling her around in a tight hug.

"Yeah! See that, Aiden. Becca knows about the sharing is caring rule." He presses a hard kiss on her cheek and squeezes her tight. "You know what, Princess? I've decided we've gotta keep ya. Our family could use a sweet female around." Setting her down on her feet, he pats her bottom and kisses his teeth with an approving nod. "This one is definitely a keeper, bro. I'm giving you a fair warning. If you set her loose, I'm chasing after this one."

Laughing, Rebecca walks back into Aiden's arms and pretends to curtsy. "Thanks for your approval, Max."

I really do love the banter between these two. Their camaraderie is incredible. From what I've seen so far, I'd love to be part of their family – if only I was given a real chance. Unfortunately, this will likely only last for the next month. Unless, of course, Aiden believes we're worthy of a long-term relationship, and who can honestly decide anything long-term in 30 days?

It takes Lance about an hour to complete the paperwork and clear Aiden's cheque. Once it's finally done, he hands Rebecca the ownership and keys to her brand new metallic red convertible. Aiden may have written the cheque, but the ownership is in her name, free and clear.

Oh my god! I can't believe it's really mine!

As she sinks into her new car, Aiden leans on the driver's door and runs his finger under the strap of her tank top. "Why don't we stop for lunch? Obviously, we'll be looking for someplace that offers casual dining," he smirks.

"How about the Purple Lion? I'm pretty sure Emma's working, and I'd really love to show her my new car." She puts her hands together in prayer, peering up through her lashes with a big smile. "Please."

Max taps her passenger door. "Do they serve food and beer?"

"Mmhmm," she nods.

"That's good enough for me!" Hopping into the passenger seat of her car, Max slaps the dash. "Well, what are we waiting for? Let's go. If Emma is anything like you, I'll have her for lunch since all of a sudden, Aiden forgot how to share." He waggles his brows with a sly smile.

Aiden's voice is deep and commanding as he shoots him a dirty look. "Get the fuck out of her car, Max. You can drive your damn self."

Max tilts his head, sticking his bottom lip out at Aiden. "Aw, are you afraid I'll steal your lady, bro?' Cause with that attitude, you should be."

Storming over to the passenger side, Aiden opens the door and grabs him by the arm. "All right, Max. That's enough. Get out of the fucking car."

"I guess I'll meet you there, Princess," Max laughs, stepping out as he blows her a kiss.

She shakes her head, looking up at Aiden. "Are you going to follow me, or am I going to follow you?"

"You lead the way," he says, leaning in to give her a kiss.

Watching in her rear-view mirror, she catches a glimpse of Aiden and Max playing musical lanes behind her. *Damn, these two can be so childish – I love it!*

They pull into the parking lot at the Purple Lion, and Max parks so tight against the driver's door of Aiden's car that he has no choice but to move or climb out the passenger side. As stubborn as Aiden is, he struggles to pull his big body across the center console, trying to get to the passenger door. They laugh as they watch him periodically shake his fist at Max and call out threats until he finally kicks open the passenger door. "I'm only going to put up with so much, Max. For this little stunt, lunch is on you. I'll have one of everything on the fucking menu!"

"Yeah yeah! Why didn't you just choose another spot,"

Max laughs. "Anyway, you're out now. Let's go. You've pissed around so much it's almost supper time, for christ's sake." Uncrossing his ankles, Max drops his arms from his chest and shakes his head. "Seriously, Princess, how do you put up with his whining?"

Smiling, Rebecca walks over to Aiden and slings her arm through his. "You two are bloody hilarious. I can't imagine what you must have put your poor parents through while you were growing up."

"You mean our poor Grandparents. Our parents have been dead since we were eight. Aiden didn't tell you," Max asks, throwing his arm over her shoulder as they walk into the bar.

Aiden shakes his head, lifting Max's arm from her shoulder and replaces it with his own. "No. It's not really something that has come up till now."

Great! Foot meet mouth.
"God. I'm so sorry, guys," she says, pulling her foot from her mouth.

Max shrugs. "Meh, don't be. It was for the best. Besides, they aren't technically dead," he says, using his fingers as quotations. "They're just dead to us." Smiling, he claps his hands. "All right, that's enough of that dreary shit. This growing boy needs food and beer!"

Emma anxiously darts toward them, her face flushed and eyes wide. "Hey, Becca. I don't finish until six, and um, I'm not sure you'll want to be here right now anyway." She waves her arm toward the bar. "Alex and the band are here. Maybe you and Aiden should go somewhere else for now. I can't have you guys fighting here. I mean, you know how much I need this job."

"Relax, Em. We have no intention of fighting." Rebecca turns back to gain confirmation from Aiden and Max. "Right, guys?" Both brothers stand with their arms folded and nod. "See. We just came to have some lunch, and I wanted to show you my new car." She grabs hold of Emma's arm, turning her toward the guys. "Oh, and I wanted to introduce you to Max, Aiden's twin brother. Max, this is my best friend and roommate, Emma."

Max nods. *I'll be polite for your sake, princess, but there's something about the way she lifted herself off that guy at the bar and sprinted toward us that doesn't sit well with me. In fact, there is something about this girl that I simply don't like.* Rebecca's voice breaks through his thoughts. "Since Max is starving, why don't you two go grab us a table and order while I show Em my car?"

Nodding, Aiden smiles, kissing her on the forehead. "Sure, baby. Don't be long."

Max's gaze is still anchored on Emma when Aiden takes his seat at an empty table. He shakes his head, waving him over. "Yo, Max. What's with you? You want to go with the girls, or do you want to get a beer and order some food?"

As Rebecca and Emma reach the parking lot, Emma's jaw drops. "Holy sheep shit, Becca! Aiden bought you this?"

Dancing around the car as if she were a teenager, Rebecca's face lights up. "I know, right! Isn't it amazing, Em! I fucking love it!"

"Yeah, that's a pretty sweet ride. What did you have to do for it, Becca?" Alex's voice resonates from behind her like a foghorn.

"Alex! Stop!" Emma slams into him, trying to shove him back toward the building. "Just go back inside! You promised you wouldn't cause a scene."

"No, Em, *you* go inside. This doesn't concern you." Pushing Emma aside, he continues toward Rebecca until he's standing directly in front of her. His angry eyes digging deep into her soul. His lips stretch across his teeth as he lowers his tone. "I said, go inside, Emma. I need to talk to Becca – alone."

Rebecca turns her head to watch Emma run inside, and she's praying Aiden sees her come in alone. She steps back, trying to manoeuvre around Alex, but he moves with her, backing her against the car. "Why don't you take me for a drive," he says, his arms caging her in as he leans over, placing his hands on the hood. "You know, you can show me how this baby handles." He doesn't sound at all like Alex – not the Alex she knew. This Alex is scary with crazy eyes and an ominous undertone.

Rebecca sees the bar doors swing open and two big bodies strutting their way. Their body language says they're not very happy and a quick glance at their faces tells her they're rather pissed. Still, Alex's eyes never budge from hers. Not even when Aiden's deep voice calls out to her, "Are you okay, baby?"

Before she can reply, Alex spits back, "She's fine, Daddy Warbucks. Mind your business. We're fucking talking."

Aiden's steps quicken, and before Rebecca realizes it, he's standing next to her. "That question wasn't directed at you. Now was it, rockstar?"

Max grabs Alex by the scruff of the neck, dragging him back as Aiden draws Rebecca in tight to his chest. He brushes the hair from her cheek and kisses her forehead. "Are you okay? Did he touch you?"

A loud bang echoes behind her, and she doesn't realize until she hears Max growl that it's the impact of Alex's head against the hood of Aiden's car. "I think you missed it when Becca said she didn't want to talk to you anymore."

"Fuck off, you bohemian!" Alex snarls back, trying to kick out of Max's grip. "She's mine. We had a disagreement and need to sort some things out, that's all. Tell them, Becca."

Mine?!

Rebecca's fear turns to anger as she twists out of Aiden's arms and stands in front of Alex with flared nostrils. "Yours?! I'm not yours, Alex! We haven't been dating in over a year. We agreed to stay in touch when you left, but that never happened. Did it? In fact, I haven't spoken to you in a year, and the only time I've seen you is when you've had some tramp draped over you. I have no interest in you or your lifestyle." She flings her arm back toward Aiden. "I'm with Aiden now. So get fucking used to it!"

I know it might only be for 30 days, but that doesn't mean I'll be going back to him!

Max pulls Alex back, tightening his grip. "Now, did you hear the lady that time?"

"Yeah, I fucking heard her!"

Max lets him go, and Alex straightens, staring at Rebecca.

His earlier anger now displaced, leaving something resembling hurt. "Real nice, Becca. I thought we were a team, you and me. We were supposed to get married." He starts walking toward the bar. "What happened to all that, huh," he yells, glancing back over his shoulder. His hand comes to rest on the door handle, and he stands staring at her for a moment. Then, pulling the door open, he chucks his chin at her and yells, "Hey, Becca, just tell me one thing. Are you at least thinking of me when he's fucking you?"

Gasping, Rebecca folds herself into Aiden's chest as Alex shakes his head and walks into the bar.

"Wow, now that was a dramatic exit," Max says, folding his arms across his chest as he watches the bar doors close.

Aiden wraps his arms around her. "Don't let him get to you, baby. He clearly has some issues to work through." Then, lifting her head, he kisses her on the cheek. "Now, we have a table full of food in there, and I'm pretty sure he's not going to be sticking around to bother us. So why don't we put this behind us and go eat."

Max strolls up beside them and gently pats her on the back with a shake of his head. "Yeah, can you believe this stupid fucker really ordered one of everything on the god damn menu?"

Rebecca tilts her head as she peers up at Aiden. "Seriously?"

"Let's go see," he shrugs.

When they get back inside, Rebecca notices their one

table has turned into three, filled with plates of food Aiden ordered. She shakes her head with a chuckle. "I can't believe you really did it."

"Oh, please. Max had it coming," he says, pulling out her chair. "Here, have a seat. Your friend's coming with the rest."

Emma saunters over and drops another plate with a pathetic attempt at a sympathetic smile. Then, throwing her arms around Rebecca, she squeezes her tight. "I'm so sorry, Becca. I tried to warn you. Alex hasn't been himself all morning."

Rebecca lets her off way too easy for Max's liking with her meek and mild response. "It's fine. It's not your fault, Em."

"No no," Max says, grabbing Emma's arm as she attempts to walk away. "Actually, Em," he says, putting a strong emphasis on her abbreviated name. "Don't you think you should tell Becca the real reason you tried to get her to leave when we came in? You know, since she's your best friend and all."

Rebecca's brows draw together as she peers at Max, holding Emma back as she shakes her head. "I don't know what you're talking about," Emma says quickly.

Her voice just went up an octave with that quick response, and she's fighting to get the hell away from me. There's no fucking way she doesn't know what I'm talking about.
Max raises his brow. "Oh, no?" Becca glances between Max and Emma, waiting to see where is going with this. "You see, Becca, now that I know who Alex is and heard what he had to say, I can tell you that this little number isn't much of a friend." He chucks his chin at Emma. "Still

nothing? Okay, well, weren't you the one that unlocked your tongue from Alex as we walked in and scurried over to us? Isn't that the real reason you tried to push Becca back out the door so quickly?"

Her face turns deep cherry, and she drops her head in her hands. "Becca, I... He was upset. God. I'm so sorry."

Rebecca closes her eyes, absorbing the new information, then lifts her chin and forces a smile. "Honestly, I don't care about Alex. He can do what he likes. We haven't been together for a long time." Narrowing her eyes, she bites her cheek. "But you, you were my best friend. I loved you and trusted you with every little detail." She shakes her head. "I would have never thought you, of all people, would go for my leftovers. Especially when you knew the way he treated me. For that, you two deserve each other." Emma tries to speak, but Rebecca puts her hand up, dismissing her. "Don't! I don't care, Em. Just keep him out of my room until I can move my stuff out of the house and enjoy your misery."

Dropping her eyes to the floor, Emma keeps her head low as she turns and walks back toward the kitchen.

Max's eyes soften as he peers over at Rebecca. "I'm really sorry, Princess, but I couldn't allow them to dog you like that." Forcing a smile, Rebecca nods, and that's good enough for Max.

Leaving a ton of food behind, Aiden is about to leave a tip when Max stops him. "Really, dude? I don't care how big the mess is today – no tip."

Aiden nods, winking down at Rebecca. "Okay, well, Natasha has a wardrobe coming within a couple of days, but we can swing by your place to grab an outfit or two if you'd like."

She smiles. "Yes, please."

"Great! I have nothing better to do," Max says. "I'll follow you two."

Thankful that no one is there, Rebecca leads them up to her room so they can wait while she grabs a few things. When she opens the door, Max is like a teenage boy. He immediately flops down on her bed, crosses his ankles and clasps his hands behind his head. Aiden barely enters her room. Instead, he leans against the doorframe, impatiently waiting with his arms folded and watches her as she moves about the room. She's been back and forth from the bathroom to the closet and the dresser, packing things for about 20 minutes when Aiden rolls his head against the frame and groans. "Come on, baby. Just grab a couple outfits and maybe a spare bathing suit. I told you, Natasha has already ordered you a complete wardrobe. It will likely be delivered to the house by tomorrow." He raises two fingers. "Two days tops."

She turns around, shifts her weight to one leg and places her hand on her hip. "I don't need a whole new wardrobe, Aiden. I have clothes."

Propping himself up on his elbows, Max shakes his head. "Becca, Becca, Becca. Let him buy the damn clothes." His eyes work their way from her calves to her face, finally settling on her eyes. "If Natasha picked out what you're wearing now." He clicks his tongue, and with a slight turn of his head, he winks. "Please. Let him buy the damn clothes."

Narrowing his eyes, Aiden chucks his chin. "I think it's time for you to go home, Maxwell."

Letting out a hearty laugh, Max lifts himself from the bed. "Yeah, you're right. It is time for me to head out. I've got some shit to do." He raises his hand and winks at Rebecca. "See you later, princess." He whacks Aiden on the back. "Latez, bro."

Chapter 6 – The Messy Maiden

When they arrive at Aiden's, Rebecca kicks her shoes off and flops down on the sofa, her eyes following Aiden as he walks over to his desk. Pulling out a manilla folder, he retrieves a piece of paper and hands her a copy of the last page of their contract. "I believe I owe you an item."

Handing her a glass of wine, he sits across from her and rests his ankle over his knee. "Now, be sure to choose wisely, Rebecca. You only get one."

She glances down at the page, the multiple-choice page she skimmed past, and immediately spots a word that sends chills up her spine.
'Anal'
Is he fucking serious?
Heat creeps across her cheeks as she peers up at him through her brows. "Um, Aiden—"

A sly smile spreads across his lips as he raises his glass to his mouth and takes a generous drink.
I knew she would try for more once she had a good look at that page. I have no intention of doing half of those things, but I'm certainly not going to tell her that.

"Rebecca, I'm being a gentleman by offering you one item." Dropping his resting foot from his knee, he sits forward. "You know, you really should consider this a privilege, Miss D'Angelo. Let's not forget this contract has already been agreed to." He smirks, slowly articulating his next words, "As a successful businessman, I don't renegotiate contracts – not once they've been signed." He sets his glass down on the table beside him and clasps his hands on the arms of his chair. His eyes narrow as he watches her contemplate her options. Releasing a breath, he smiles, his tone somewhat impatient as he leans forward, running his hand along the side of his face. "Honestly, I see no reason why you can't leave it open. I have no issues with being able to explore freely." He stands, fanning his hands out in front of him. "I mean, after all, I'm not a brute. I'm sure you must know by now that my intention is not to hurt you."

I know he has no intention of hurting me, but really, Aiden? Anal?
"Aiden, there's a whole section dedicated to Anal alone!" She stares at him, her eyes almost pleading. "If I check off the anal heading, does that cancel all of the items listed under that section?"
I know I sound like I'm whining, I am, and I don't care.

A smirk graces his face as he walks over to sit beside her on the sofa. "Is that honestly your biggest fear," he asks, taking the paper from her hands and holding it up to examine it.

She shrugs. "I'm not sure. I still haven't read the whole damn thing. I just know that the thought of anal scares the hell out of me."
The craziest part is, it kind of excites me too. I can feel that annoying little pulse between my thighs when I think of it. In fact, I am almost certain if I were to check my panties, they would probably be damp. But that's definitely not something

I'm going to tell him. I can explore that when I'm ready, not at his whim.

Aiden tosses the paper to the floor like it's trash. "This thing is useless anyway if you really think about it." Her eyes grow wide as they follow the page to the floor. She's about ready to freak out when she decides to sit back and wait for his explanation instead. She stares at him doubtingly, yet curious to see where he's going with this. He brushes the hair back from her cheek. "Look, let's be completely honest here. You don't even know your limits. So why don't we forget about that page, and we can learn your limits together?"

Taking a deep breath, the corner of her mouth tightens as she nods. "Okay, I suppose I can live with that solution." Then suddenly, that word flashes before her eyes again.

'Anal'

"Wait, but that doesn't—"

He gently places his finger over her lips and smiles. "Shhh." Kissing her lightly on the forehead, he walks back over to the bar. As he picks up the bottle of wine, he peers up at her through his brow. "We can gently explore *all* your limits, Rebecca." A slight smirk settles on his lips as he finishes filling his glass and peers up at her. "You have my word that I would never put you in danger or harm you in any way, but you should know that I will test your limits from time to time."

Come on, Becca, swallow. You were born with the ability. It's a natural god damn reflex. You can do it.

Emptying her wine glass in one swallow, she holds it up to Aiden. His brow shooting up with his chuckle. "Are you thirsty?"

Trying to digest the wild images surfacing from his previous statement, she clears her throat and forces a smile. "Mmhmm, maybe a little."

Aiden waves her over to the bar. "I hate seeing you this uneasy. Why don't you come join me? Let me teach you my secrets to making the best ice cream floats," he winks. "I promise, you'll never think of them the same again."

As Rebecca walks up beside him, he swoops down, playfully grabbing her by the waist and lifts her into the air — her laughter filling the room as he sets her on the bar. "Jesus, Aiden," she squeals.

"You're fine. I've got you. Just lean back and hold the rail," he says, gesturing to the brass bar behind her. As his laughter fades to a soft chuckle, his warm breath feathers across her neck, and he runs his hands lightly over her hips to her inner thighs. Slowly spreading her legs, he stands between them as his eyes scan her body, his sly smile one of approval. "There, now that's perfect. Stay just like that." Reaching under the bar, he pulls out a pair of scissors and Rebecca's heart begins to race.

She bounds forward, closing her legs against his waist. "What the fuck, Aiden?!"

He places his hand against her chest. "Rebecca, please. I've already assured you I wouldn't do anything to hurt you. I'm a man of my word, but if you're not going to do as I ask" – a smirk forms on his lips as he tips his head – "I won't hesitate to tie you in place. His eyes soften as he peers down at her heaving chest. He cups her chin in his hand, giving her a reassuring kiss. "I promise you're going to love this. Now, please, go back to your position."

Unsure how this man can have such an effect on her, she tries to ignore the twitch between her thighs and focuses on repositioning herself as he asked. Grabbing the rail, she spreads her legs and looks up at him. "But I thought we were making ice cream floats."

"Don't worry, we will," he says, meticulously running the scissors along the outside of her shorts. "I need to prepare a couple of things first."

She watches him carefully slip his finger under the waistband of her shorts and slide it to one side, holding the material out from her body. Cold metal glides along her outer thigh as he slices through the seam, and she sucks in her stomach with a gasp. "What the hell, Aiden? These are new!"

"Relax, I'll buy you another pair." Then, making two final snips through the waistband, he stands back with a satisfied grin. "Besides, Max enjoys these on you a little too much."

Closing her eyes, Rebecca leans back as Aiden repeats the process on the opposite side and flips the front panel of her shorts forward. She raises her head and bites down on her bottom lip to keep from shrieking as he lifts the elastic on her panties from her hip. Snipping each side, he lets them fall between her thighs. Rebecca's stomach twists; she takes a deep breath, trying her best to remain still and silent.

As the scissors slice through the hem of her tank top, Rebecca's quick intake of breath causes Aiden to peer up through his brows. He lowers the scissors and tilts his head. "Honestly, Rebecca. Will you please try to trust me?"

"I do. I'm sorry." Her head falls back, and she closes her eyes, expelling a breath through tight lips. "Go ahead. I'll stay still."

A couple more snips, and he severs her tank top and bra, exposing her chest to the chill of the evening air. Her nipples quickly respond, almost stinging as they harden, sending a message directly to her core. Leaving every sensitive nerve on high alert, she inhales as the last stitch of material slides from her shoulders.

As Aiden shifts, she opens her eyes, her body igniting under his stare as his eyes travel her body. Nodding, he smiles. "Mmm, there we go. Now, *that's* better."

He leans down, his face only inches from her flesh as he maintains the pace of a well-rehearsed adagio working his way across her body. Goosebumps push to the surface, sending explicit messages through every cell. Her breath catches, and the tip of his nose grazes her pebbled nipple. A slight, 'ah' leaves her lips as her head rolls to the side, but he doesn't falter. Instead, the soft touch of his fingers trail sluggishly along her thighs. He kisses the base of her neck, the middle, then behind her ear. Then all contact disappears, and she opens her eyes, staring up at a cunning smile.

"Oh, don't look so disappointed, Rebecca. We've only just begun."

Her lids heavy, she tries to focus on his hand as it cups her mound. As he slips a finger between her folds, she draws a breath, pressing her hips forward. His light eyes darken, and he slowly pulls his hand back with a smile. "See that? We're making new discoveries about what you like every day." He licks the length of his finger with a moan. "Damn, there really is nothing like the taste of a woman's arousal."

Her body feeling the void of his touch, she takes a deep breath and straightens, making Aiden chuckle. "Don't worry, we'll come back to that. You distracted me. I almost forgot," he winks. "We're making ice cream floats" – leaning down, he kisses her – "and I'd have to say you're about the perfect temperature."

He grabs a tub of chocolate ice cream from the bar freezer and places it between her thighs with a spoon. Then, clutching two large beer mugs, he sets them down beside her. "Now, I know you have other things on that pretty little mind of yours, but try to pay attention. I think you're really going to like this."

A little disappointed, she relaxes and watches him scoop ice cream into the two mugs, counting as he goes. "One for you... One for me... Two for you... Two for me..." He glances up at her with his sly grin in place, then scoops ice cream onto the top of her bare mound.

Stiffening, her eyes widen as she gasps, "Holy shit, Aiden!"

He places his hands on her thighs, laughing as he holds her steady. "Easy now, that one is for us."

Breathing in deep through her nose, she peers up at him. "That's bloody cold."

Still chuckling, Aiden nods. "Of course, it's ice cream. Now stay still until I'm finished. I promise you're going to love this." He reaches for the Amaretto and pours a shot in each mug than a shot into a smaller glass. He adds a small dab of whiskey, then grabs a bottle of root beer, adding some to each mixture before focusing his eyes back on hers. "How are you doing? Still cold?"

She tips her head from side to side, crinkling her nose with a shrug. "Not really. It's mostly melted and dripping." She leans back, twisting her lips as she shows him the puddle of melted cream. "It's just messy now."

"Mmm, that it is. I think I'll have to call this the Messy Maiden." Scrunching her nose, Aiden chuckles. "Don't worry. I'm going to clean you up." He grabs the smaller glass and kneels between her thighs. "Shift your bottom forward," he says, holding the tumbler above her mound. As his tongue touches her taint, he begins to slowly pour the contents—lapping at the liquid as it drips between her folds.

Her head falls back as an airy 'Ohh' leaves her lips, and she grips his hair in her fist, pushing herself against his tongue. He drops the glass, sliding his finger inside and clears any evidence of ice cream from between her thighs. As butterflies take flight in her stomach, a beautiful burst of nervous excitement shakes her body. He holds her hips firmly, delving deep into her opening with his sinful tongue, and slowly coaxes out every last wave of her orgasm.

Hovering above her, he wipes the moisture from his face with the back of his hand – the corner of his mouth lifting into a smile. "You can be honest. What do you think of my ice cream floats?"

Smiling at his glistening face, she sits up. "Well, honestly. I love your method of delivery, and I guarantee that I will always think of this night when someone mentions an ice cream float from now on."

Reaching for one of the mugs, she takes a drink. "Wow, and this actually tastes really good." Aiden's smile broadens as she grabs the spoon and holds it up. "All right, come here." He leans down, and she lightly taps his head. "I, Rebecca D'Angelo, officially crown you the ice cream float king and master of orgasms," she winks.

Aiden takes the spoon from her hand and gives her a kiss. "Master, huh?" He pulls his phone from his back pocket.

Rebecca's brows draw together as her smile fades. "What are you doing?"

"Oh, Max needs to hear about this one," he says, pretending to punch numbers into his phone.

"Aiden!"

Chuckling, he closes his phone, tosses it on the bar and pulls off his t-shirt. "Don't ever think I'd call Max while you're sitting here naked." Turning his back to her, he taps his shoulder. "Come on, hop up."

She glances down at her sticky self and shakes her head. "Nah-uh. I'm naked and sticky. That's gross."

He turns around, shaking his head as he rolls his eyes. "Okay, this is me. I'm not the one to be a prude with. Might I remind you I've been inside that body – made it quiver like a newborn calf trying to gain his legs." With a snap of his head, he pats his back. "Now, let's go. Get up here."

Giggling, she wraps herself around him and kisses his neck. "Oh, you have such a way with words, Mr. Collins." Then, tightening her arms around his chest, she rests her cheek against his back. "Should I ask where you're taking me?"

Stopping to slide open the patio doors, he glances over his shoulder. "Where else? To the hot tub so you can warm up." Crouching next to the tub, he sets her down and flicks the switch. She leans over, watching as the water comes to life with colour while Aiden undoes his jeans and adjusts the temperature. "The lights are still going to be there when you get in, Rebecca," he smirks.

She climbs in, her eyes following Aiden as he walks over to the bar. He's tanned, he's muscular, he's perfection wrapped up in a big beautiful frame – he's everything a girl wants when she steps into a man's arms. She bites down on her finger, watching as his tattoos waltz gracefully across his back and wonders if he planned them that way. Then, thankful she's in water, she takes a deep breath and sinks a little deeper.

God, help me! I'm in way, way over my head.

Aiden struts back to the hot tub carrying two glasses and a bottle of whiskey under his arm. Wiggling his hips, he lets his jeans drop around his ankles and steps in the tub with a smile. "All right, I thought we'd have a couple shots of whiskey tonight." He sets their glasses down on the edge of the tub and pours them each a shot. Sealing up the bottle, he drops it into the waves and hands her a glass. "To trying new things and keeping an open mind."

Rebecca giggles as images of the last few days flash through her mind. "How about just to us," she asks.

With a tight smile, Aiden gives her a curt nod and clanks his glass to hers. "Yes, of course. To us."

Tipping back the glass of liquid hell, she can feel it burn the entire way to her stomach. "Holy shit! That's just as bad as the tequila," she says between breaths, handing him back the glass.

Laughing, he fishes the bottle out to refill their glasses. Pouring them each another round, he raises his glass to clink it with hers, his face taking on a more serious look. "Now, this is to *discovering* us."

Rebecca's face softens as she nods, inviting the liquid fire into her mouth. She waits for it to hit bottom and blows out the burn. Relieving her of her glass, Aiden takes her hand. "That stuff will definitely warm you from the inside out, but I have something else I'd like to offer that may be a little more inviting. "Come here," he says, pulling her onto his lap. His kiss is filled with a promise of incredible passion as he positions her on top of him. She slowly lowers and lifts, easing him inside until she's finally resting firmly against his groin. Closing her eyes, she inhales.

He grabs her hips and grinds himself into her while his tongue slips past her lips. Right or wrong, this is the side of Aiden Collins she'd sign a lifetime contract for.

Her stomach tenses with excitement, every muscle tightening in protest as his pace quickens. His breathing increases as his fingers dig into her bottom, pulling her down with every upward thrust. Her legs tremble as his girth seems to expand, and she grips his shoulders, releasing a moan. He drives himself deep as the tension of her imminent orgasm continues to build – she's looking down the first big hill of a rollercoaster, and it's about to plunge. He lifts her bottom, powering into her with a roar and the rush of heat floods her body. The breath she was unaware was being held now spills out in broken syllables, "Oh – my – god yes."

Aiden's moan comes from somewhere deep inside as he wraps his arms around her waist and pulls her tight against his chest. "Fuck, baby, you're going to be my demise."

Giving him a kiss, she runs her fingers through his damp hair. "Mmm, I hope not. You're kind of growing on this messy maiden."

She stands, freeing herself from his lap and the hot tub while he watches her every move. "You know, it's only seven-thirty. Feel like taking in the aquarium? We might be able to catch the final octopus show before it closes," he says, stepping out of the tub.

"Yeah, I love the aquarium! Just let me go get dressed."

Rebecca hurries upstairs and slips the cute peach-coloured sundress over her head. Remembering Aiden prefers her hair down, she leaves it loose across her shoulders and quickly touches up her makeup. As she takes a minute to examine herself in the mirror, she catches a glimpse of him stalking up behind her. His arms slink around her waist, and he nestles his chin into her neck. "You look beautiful. Let's go, or we'll miss the aquarium," he says, leaving a light kiss behind her ear.

She spins around to face him, taking in his relaxed appearance. *He's wearing slim-fitting black dress pants and a white polo shirt, showing just the right amount of his best assets. His hair is finger tousled, in that sexy 'I don't give a fuck' kind of way and the smell of him – he's almost edible.* She wraps her arms around his waist and kisses his neck. "Mmm, I could smell you all day."

Taking her hand, he leads her from the bathroom. "Somehow, I doubt it would stop at a smell. Let's go before we miss the aquarium, my insatiable little monster."

She steps back, her mouth slack as she holds her hand to her chest. "Are you complaining, Mr. Collins? Because I'm pretty sure you woke this monster, and correct me if I'm wrong, but it didn't sound or feel like you were complaining a few minutes ago in the hot tub."

Chuckling, he pulls her into his arms. "Rebecca, I would never complain of such a thing. That was meant to be an endearment, not an insult." Kissing her on the forehead, he taps her bottom and turns her toward the front door. "Now, let's get going."

They make it to the aquarium a half hour before it closes and just in time to catch the tail end of the final performance for the octopus tank. After the performance, they spend a few minutes handling the starfish, then head into the gift shop for a few souvenirs. "Are you hungry?"

Bouncing on the balls of her feet, she takes his hand, pulling him toward the street vendors. "Mmhmm, I could use a hotdog."

"A hotdog?" He sounds as if she just asked him for an old

tire.

"Yeah! The hotdog cart on Beacon Avenue is the best."

He shoves his hands in his front pockets stubbornly as they stand in front of the hotdog cart on Beacon Avenue. "I was thinking maybe Haro's or the Waterfront Grill."

She tucks her arms through his and looks up into his eyes. "Loosen up, baby. Try a hotdog, please."

A smile graces his lips as he nods. "All right, but only because you called me baby and on one condition." He leans in close to her ear. "When we get home, you let me see if that cute little ass of yours truly is off-limits."

Whoa! I wasn't expecting that.
"Aiden—"

"Now now, Rebecca." He gives her a stern look as he pulls his hands from his pockets and places them on her upper arms. "Tit for tat. You promised to open yourself up and try new things. I'm agreeing to do the same thing by ingesting street meat."

Rebecca shifts her weight with a huff. "Aiden, that's not even remotely the same! You're asking me to introduce a foreign object into a body cavity that's not designed for such a violation."

Chuckling, he shakes his head. "Street meat is foreign to my body and a complete violation to my digestive tract. I'd consider it the same thing other than the end it's entering. Besides, anal is quite common between two consenting adults."

Pursing her lips, she anchors her hand on her hip. "I can't

believe you just said that! Eating one hotdog will not hurt you" – her brows raise – "stuffing your dick in my ass, however," She takes a breath looking up at the shocked patrons around them and lowers her voice. "I'm sorry, but I've heard that it can be rather painful."

The realization of her true fear flashes in his eyes, and his face softens. "Fine, I'll eat the damn hotdog. But I've proved myself to you by now, Rebecca. I will not do anything to hurt you." He turns back to face the vendor with a smile and puts two fingers in the air as if he's done it a million times. "We'll have two footlongs, please."

Rebecca glares up at him as he shrugs. "Okay, fine. I may enjoy the odd hotdog from time to time, but given the option of Haro's or street meat—" He shakes his head with a slight smile. "No one in their right mind except you would choose a damn hotdog."

Her shoulders relax as she chuckles, retrieving their hotdogs from the vendor. "I happen to like them." She squeezes mustard across them and hands one to Aiden.

Glancing at her, he smirks. "Yes, clearly."

Walking toward the pier, they pass the fish market and glass beach. Aiden stops to stand by the famous wooden scuba diver, appeasing her while taking a few pictures with her phone. She picks some flowers from the nearby garden and places them in the curled hand of the statue of the old man sitting on the bench. She toes some gravel and looks around. Other than an older couple crab fishing over the edge of one of the fishing balconies, it seems they'll be alone on the pier. Aiden takes her hand as they casually stroll toward the end. There's no moon or stars in the sky. Aside from a couple of flashing lights marking random boats moving in and out of the harbour, it's pitch black. A cold breeze whips Rebecca's hair into her face, and she flicks it back, folding her arms across her chest. "Brrr, it's gotten chilly since we left the house."

Aiden rubs her back and arms, trying to warm her. "I wasn't thinking. We should have brought you a sweater. Why don't we head back to the car? It's getting late anyway." Rebecca nods, sliding in under his arm. As they near the last fishing balcony, she spots Alex and his drummer Johnny sitting on the bench. She lowers her head, pretending not to notice when Aiden stops and points them out. "Hey, isn't that Alex and his buddy?"

"Um, yeah, I think it is." Tugging him forward, she continues toward the end of the pier. "Can we just go, please?"

Aiden pulls her to a halt only a few feet from where Alex and his friend are sitting. He lifts her chin and gazes down. "I don't want you to worry about him, not when you're with me. I promise I won't let anyone bother you." He kisses her forehead and swoops down, unexpectedly lifting her into his arms with a loud burst of laughter.

"Jesus, Aiden!" She swats his chest, trying to pull back her smile. "I didn't want him to know we were here."

"I want him to know. Let him see that he has no effect on us – that it's you and me now."

Rebecca forces a smile as she scans his face and nods. Her mind trying to make sense of his words, *'you and me now.'* Does he mean that, or does he mean *'for now?'*

When they reach the edge of the walkway, Aiden sets her

on her feet and spins her to face him. Resting his hand against her neck, he gently sweeps his thumb across her cheek. "You do know that you're safe with me, right?"

Nodding, she meets his eyes. "I do. I just don't like conflict."

Kissing her, he takes her by the hand. "Of course, nor do I. Now, what do you say I take you home so we can get you warmed up?"

She smiles, but the nagging thought of what will happen after 30 days plagues her as they head for the car.
Is it really enough time for him to make a love connection?
Should I stop myself from falling for him?
Is he even capable of true love?

On the way back to his house, she has to ask. He seems to be lost in his own thoughts as she peers over at him and lays her hand in his lap. "Aiden?"

"Mmhmm."

She lays her head against the headrest and faces him. "What's going to happen when the 30 days are up?" She watches for any sign that might give away his true feelings, but he remains focused on the road.

"What exactly do you mean, Rebecca? I thought all expectations were clearly defined in the contract. Didn't we discussed it in depth over lunch?" Finally, he glances over with his brows drawn together. "Is there something wrong?"

Feeling the heat creep across her cheeks, she shakes her head. "No, there's nothing wrong. I just wish this wasn't based on a contract—a time frame. I keep seeing the sand sliding through the hourglass and wondering if 30 days is" – she pauses and looks out her window to avoid his gaze – "well if love is even possible in 30 days."

He reaches into his lap and takes her hand in his. "Rebecca, love can't be defined by time. You could fall in love with someone in a moment." He squeezes her hand and smiles. "Let's try and forget about the contract for now, okay? I'm genuinely enjoying my time with you. So, let's concentrate on the here and now and let things fall into place."

Forcing a light smile, she nods. "Okay."

Max's Hummer is parked in the driveway when they arrive at the house, and Aiden groans at its sight. Frowning, he takes a deep breath. "I had no idea he was going to be here tonight. I'll get rid of him," he says, turning off the car.

"No, it's fine. I don't mind Max being here. He doesn't bother me." She smiles, recalling their banter earlier this afternoon. "I like him. He brings out the real Aiden."

Aiden shakes his head. "I'm not convinced you'd like the real Aiden. I'm trying really hard to be different with you, Rebecca." With a quick kiss, he gets out of the car and kicks Max's tire. "But, this asshole is making it extremely fucking difficult."

Getting out of the car, Rebecca laughs. "Do you feel better now?"

He throws his arm around her shoulder with a smile and nods. "Yes. I kind of do." He kisses her forehead. "Let's go see what he wants so we can get rid of him. Shall we?"

Chapter 7 — Surprise!

As Max leaves Rebecca's house, one thought continuously runs through his mind...

I'm done watching Aiden act all prim and proper. She's not one of our associates. How dare he have this little princess all to himself? I can feel it. She's the one we've always talked about – waited for. That one girl that can satisfy both our needs and still ask for more. I can see it in her eyes – her body language.
She's hungry.
She's the perfect mix of good and bad, and I need a fucking taste.

With the arrangements made, Max slips into his Hummer and heads over to Aiden's to spring his plan into action. When he pulls into the driveway, Aiden's car is gone, but that's never stopped him before. He lets himself in and slides on the pair of Lycra swim shorts he keeps there – the ones Aiden hates. Diving into the pool, he swims a few laps and waits. As suspected, only a few laps in, and he lifts his head to Aiden and Rebecca standing at the end of the pool watching him. He leaps out, standing only inches from Rebecca's side and offers a smile. "Hey, guys! I got tired of waiting, so I thought I'd take a dip."

His smile broadens as Rebecca's stare trails down his body.

That's right, baby.
I knew you were hungry.

Aiden raises his brow at Rebecca, tossing Max a towel. "What are you doing here? We weren't expecting company tonight, Max. We were down at the pier when Rebecca caught a chill." He pulls her protectively against his side. "We were just about to have a warm bath and head to bed."

Max laughs inwardly at Aiden's greedy actions.
Yeah, great idea, but I don't fucking think so, bro!

Placing her hand on Aiden's arm, she peers up at him. "Actually, I'm okay. I warmed up on our way home in the car."

Watching Aiden's jaw clench, Max smiles.
Aw, not what you wanted her to say, bro? God, I love this girl!

Flashing Aiden his biggest shit-eating grin he can muster, Max slaps him on the back. "Great! Then why don't you two get your swimsuits on and meet me in the hot tub? I have a surprise for you both." He gives Rebecca a wink. "The hot tub will warm you up anyway, Princess."

Narrowing his eyes, Aiden groans, reluctantly releasing Rebecca from his arm and points at Max. "Fine, but this better be worth my sacrifice."

"Come on, Aiden." Max places his hands on his hips and shakes his head. "Jesus, you need to loosen the fucking leash a bit, bro."

Flipping him the bird, Aiden disappears into the house behind Rebecca.

While they're changing, Max grabs some glasses and a

bottle of champagne, making sure the envelopes are next to the tub. He can't wait to see their reaction. Especially Aiden's when he tells them he's booked them a three-week vacation at one of the hottest adult resorts in Montego Bay.

Max sits in the hot tub and stews...

Aiden will know precisely what's on my mind. He doesn't know that I've seen his little contract yet, but he will. The fact that he didn't intend to ever share Becca with me pisses me off. He thought I would be in Seattle the entire time and be none the wiser. Just for that reason alone, he's lucky I don't take her away and keep her for myself. He's lucky I'm a fair man. I don't mind sharing like we originally planned, but — now we do it my way.

The opportunities in Jamaica to bring our dream to fruition are plentiful, and no ex-boyfriend to interfere.

It's perfect.

Aiden nervously paces as he watches Rebecca slip into her bikini.

What the fuck is Max scheming? I know he's pissed because I've excluded him from my relationship with Rebecca, but she's too perfect for sharing. Besides, there's no way I was going to lose her with an offer that included Max. She was timid enough with my proposal.

"Rebecca, there's something you should know," he says, running his hand through his hair. Something she's already come to recognize as a tense response. "Max and I have shared women many times in the past," he says in a low voice.

Her reaction is not at all what he expects. She doesn't pitch a fit or shy away. In fact, she barely acknowledges what he's said. Instead, she places her hand on her hip, drawing her brows together. "That's nice, Aiden, but I didn't see your brother's name on our contract. So obviously, that doesn't apply to me. Now, does it?"

Aiden shakes his head. "No, you're right. It doesn't apply to our agreement. I'm telling you so that you're not shocked by our history when it surfaces. I guess I'm asking you not to encourage his advances because it's becoming obvious to me that he may have the wrong idea about us."

She exhales slowly and lowers her gaze. "Can we not discuss your historical bedroom games, please. I'm sure it's as colourful as your portfolio of women."

"Rebecca, that portfolio you've brought up more than once was Max, not me. He created my social life."

Tipping her head to the side, she places her hand on her hip and stares at him. "Of course he did," she says, rolling her eyes. "God, I'd love to have a twin." Gesturing to her outfit, she shifts her weight. "I'm ready. Can we just go downstairs, please? I could really use a drink, especially now." She slips on her sandals and strides for the door.

Aiden grabs her arm, spinning her back to face him. "I'm serious, Rebecca. The photos you've seen with all those women, that's not me."

The corner of her mouth tightens as her eyes narrow. "Okay, even so. You just said yourself that you've still shared those women." She pulls her arm free and opens the door. "You know what? All of that has nothing to do with me. So let's just drop it."

When they walk out onto the patio, Rebecca notices Max's

eyes following her like a tiger stalking his prey. With Aiden's info dump still fresh in her mind, she wastes no time getting into the hot tub. She takes a seat across from Max and places her legs onto Aiden's lap. Handing her a glass of champagne, Max winks. "Here you go, princess." He chucks his chin at Aiden. "Here, bro. Fucking relax and raise your glass cause we're going to Jamaica," he hollers, holding up the three travel packages. "Woohoo! That's right. I said, Jamaica bitches! I booked us reservations at one of the most exclusive adults-only resorts in Montego Bay! We leave in 2 days."

"What?!" Aiden and Rebecca say simultaneously.

Max laughs. "Yeah! You two are just gonna kick around here and have sex all day anyway, and you'll likely keep running into Becca's ex. This is perfect. It's not like you can't have sex in Jamaica, and when you come up for air, you can have fun with me!"

Aiden purses his lips. "Fun with you, huh?"

"Yeah, Aiden. I'm actually a really fun guy."

He waves his hands toward Rebecca. "Besides, I like Becca. She deserves a real chance at happiness." He lifts his glass to Aiden and winks. "But, with this dick that dumped her suddenly coming back and trying to stake his claim. We need to take her away from this nonsense. She doesn't need that kind of bullshit. Anyway, I heard he's leaving town again in two weeks. We'll be in Montego Bay for the next three." He shrugs, taking a drink of his champagne. "Problem solved. Besides, I could use the holiday."

Aiden lifts his brow and leans back. "You sure this isn't some ploy to try and get Rebecca away from me?"

"Aiden—" Rebecca says, her voice carrying a ring of annoyance.

Max nods. "Look, I'll admit I'm a little pissed at the way you did things, but that's not what matters right now. As I see it, Rebecca is a free woman. She can make her own decisions, and I'm here to make sure she does." He directs his attention to Rebecca. "Tell me, princess. Are you happy with Montego Bay?'Cause I can take you somewhere else," he winks. "You know, leave the old man at home, and we can go anywhere your little heart desires."

"Fuck you, Maxwell," Aiden snaps, splashing water in his face. "I'm not sure what you have up your sleeve, but it better not be what I think it is."

"Lighten up, Aiden." He runs his hand down his face sweeping the water away. "My goal is to get Rebecca out of here so we can all have a good time." He shrugs. "Why not? We've earned it." He rolls his eyes cracking a smile. "Okay fine, maybe you earned it more than me. Whatever! We're still going, and we're gonna have a blast!"

Smiling, Aiden holds his hands up in front of him. "Okay, Okay! Just don't fuck with my lady." He shakes his finger. "I'm not kidding, Max."

A sly grin forms on Max's face as he raises his brow. "Shit! Your lady. Wow, Becca. What have you done to my boy?" He shakes his head in disbelief. "As I see it. It can only be one of two things. Either you're purely angelic, or you're the devil herself." Raking his eyes across her body, he chucks his chin. "So, which is it?"

Rebecca laughs nervously.

Nope. I am not biting this hook! You boys need to behave.

Looking between the two, she seems to be the only one laughing. Max appears to be waiting for a real answer while Aiden folds his arms across his chest and decides to give him one. Taking a deep breath, he puffs out his chest. "Actually, she's as pure as the undriven snow. At this point, we're making our own roads."

He looks at Rebecca and smiles. "Personally, I'd have to say we're building them somewhere between heaven and hell. Our journey so far has been pure bliss, if you must know."

Max stands with wide eyes and a slack jaw. "Wow, Aiden! That was fucking hot! Did you think that up all by yourself?" He stands and hands them both shooters. His face is still tense with expression as he stares at Aiden. "Seriously, when did you get so fucking sensitive, bro?"

Rebecca bursts out laughing. "God, Max! I feel like I was ripped off, never having a sibling like you."

Aiden throws an inflatable cushion at him, letting out a chuckle. "Shut up, man."

When the men finally settle down, Max hands them each their travel envelope. His gaze slides to Rebecca. "You do have a passport, right, Princess?" She nods, barely paying attention while checking out their travel information. "Good! Then we're set to go. We fly out the day after tomorrow." He grins at Aiden. "Oh yeah, I forgot to tell you. We're using the company jet. I had Natasha set everything up. Thanks for leaving her at my disposal. She's been amazing."

Aiden visibly tenses, and his eyes narrow at Max. "Okay, do not abuse Natasha. There is no possible way I could replace her. She could single-handedly run that company."

Rebecca's eyes shift between the two brothers. "Is this a joke? Are we actually going to Jamaica?"

Aiden pulls her into his side while Max lets out a chuckle. "Yes, baby. We are actually going to Jamaica. You know how you said you wished you had a crazy brother just like Max?" He throws his hand in the air. "It looks like he may have just claimed you." He glares at Max. "As his sister, that is. Right, Max?"

Max shrugs with a grin. "Oh, make no mistakes, princess. I am claiming you." He throws his arms out to Becca. "We're gonna make the best threesome!" His choice of words sends a shiver down Rebecca's spine, as Aiden's words playback in her mind – 'Max and I have shared women many times in the past.'

Clearing his throat, Aiden gives her a reassuring smile, then pats her bottom and gives her a slight shove toward Max's open arms. "There's so much to teach you, little one." Max takes a deep breath and pulls her into a tight embrace. "Oh, you're gonna be so much fun to party with!" He kisses the top of her head. "You know it's official now, right? You're ours! It doesn't even matter what happens with Aiden. I'm keeping you."

Taking Rebecca's hand, Aiden pulls her back into his lap. "All right, all right. Let's get a few things straight. First off, threesome was a poor choice of words. She is clearly with me. Secondly, she is not ours. Again, let me remind you. She's with me."

A mischievous grin forms on Max's face. "Whatever you say, bro." He winks and pretends to punch Rebecca's shoulder playfully, rotating his hips and dancing the best he can in a hot tub. "Don't let him scare you. We can always ditch him. Aiden might run the show here, but in Jamaica, we do what we want. In fact, I think we may need rehab by the time we get home!"

"I can't wait! I haven't been this excited since I went to Cuba with my friends on spring break. It sounds like a lot of fun!" Rebecca gives him a quick hug. "Thanks, Max."

"Anytime, princess." He looks at Aiden with a grin. "Oh, I'm gonna need one of your spare rooms tonight." He puts his hand up before Aiden can say anything. "Don't worry. I'll take the one at the opposite end of the hall. I know you haven't had a chance to soundproof the place yet." Stepping out of the tub, he pats Aiden on the back. "Now I think I've earned steak and eggs for breakfast tomorrow. Don't you?" He rubs his rock-hard abs. "I'm a growing boy, you know."

Shaking his head, Aiden smirks. "Yeah, I'll see what I can do."

"Thanks, bro." Throwing his hand up, he waves on his way into the house. "Night, Becca! Try and keep it down tonight, will ya?"

She smiles, feeling her cheeks heat. "Goodnight, Max! I'll do my best."

Rebecca is thankful Max is heading off to bed when Aiden hollers back. "Just for that, I'm going to make her moan and scream my name until you can't help but grab for the lube."

Flipping him the bird, Max disappears through the doors.

Aiden rests his arm behind her head. "Well, there you have it. There's no denying Max likes you. I'm just not convinced yet it's all brotherly."

"I think you're reading more into it than there actually is." She holds out her hand to him, showing him her pruned fingers.

"I guess we should get you out of here before you grow scales." He kisses her cheek and gives her a nudge toward the steps. "We've had enough excitement for one day anyway. Don't you think?"

"Yeah, I definitely have to agree with you there."

Max stays with them at Aiden's for the next day and a half until it's time to leave, and the dynamics of the house is unmistakably one of a tight family unit. The three of them have become inseparable.

When it's finally time to leave, the guys load their bags into Max's Hummer, and they head for the private airstrip to board the company jet for Jamaica. Rebecca sits upfront with Max and fiddles with the radio when a station announcer sings out, "We have a new song from Alex Healey this morning. Here's his newest single – Becca." The three of them grow quiet as the ballad from that first night, when Aiden had taken her to the bar, melodically begins to echo through the speakers.

The corner of Max's mouth lifts as he changes the station. "You don't need to hear that, princess. He's a fucking dog."

"You're right. Alex even said it himself. It's too little too late." A slight smile pulls at her lips as Aiden's reassuring hand lands on her shoulder. He reaches for her seatbelt and unbuckles it, gesturing for her to join him in the backseat. She climbs between the two seats landing in his lap, and wraps her arms around his neck. "I'm not going to let him or his stupid song ruin this. I've never been this happy." Her tongue sweeps across Aiden's lips as he sucks it into his mouth, taking her mind miles away from Alex Healey and anything they once had.

"Okay, you two lovebirds. As hot as that is to watch. There will be no fucking in my truck if I'm not involved," Max bellows from the front seat.

Aiden chuckles, giving her a quick smack on the bottom. "We're not fucking in your truck, but I am hoping I can convince Rebecca to join the mile high club today."

"Aiden!"

Max glances back at them through the rearview mirror. *Look how her cheeks turn bright red so quickly. Fuck she's adorable! And Aiden, such a smug prick. Making sure he rubs in his sexcapades with the little princess. That's okay, bro. Do it while you can because I guarantee I'll have a taste before this trip is over. You'll see.*

When they board the jet, Rebecca's amazed at the inside. It's like walking into an elegant mobile one-bedroom apartment. There's a lighted partition that separates the dining and sitting area. On one side, four reclining chairs surround a dining table at the front when you first enter. There is a sofa facing a credenza and flat-screen TV on the opposite side of the glass partition. Just beyond that is a bathroom, which is nothing short of spectacular. It's certainly nothing like on a commercial flight and even larger than her bathroom at home. Finally, at the very back of the plane is a bedroom with a full queen-sized bed and another built-in TV. They literally have all the luxuries of home on this plane.

She turns to look at the guys, her eyes wide. "This thing is amazing! It's like a flying apartment!"

Aiden smiles and pats Max on the back. "Yeah, it was a good call for this trip. It will be a comfortable 7-hour flight."

"I told you," Max grins with a nod. "I've got everything covered, bro. I even ordered a prime rib for dinner. We're gonna have a fucking blast!"

The pilot steps onto the plane and salutes. "Morning, gentlemen. Are you about ready to take off?"

The rest of the crew consisting of three other people, walk in behind him and smile, taking their positions. Two head into the cockpit and one into the small kitchenette. Max slaps his hand on the arm of his chair. "Andre, good buddy! We're more than ready. Take us to the fun in the sun!"

Tipping his hat, the pilot turns toward the cockpit. "Danielle will serve drinks once we reach altitude. As usual, I'm going to ask that you stay buckled up until then."

The jet engines roar to life, and within a few minutes,

the plane is racing down the runway picking up speed for takeoff. Aiden takes Rebecca's hand, lifting it to his lips. "I'll admit, I wasn't sure about this, but I'm pleased that we're taking this trip – that you're with me."

Laying her head on his shoulder, she peers up with a smile. "Me too."

When the pilot announces they've reached altitude, Max unbuckles his belt. He's decided he's not waiting for Danielle. Grabbing a bottle of whiskey and three glasses, he sets them down on the table with a wild grin. "Let's get this party started!"

Pouring them each a shot, he lifts his eyes to Rebecca. "You know, I think you're pretty special, right?"

Nodding, she accepts the glass from his hand with a warm smile. "Thanks, Max. That means a lot. I think you're really great too."

Handing Aiden his glass, he returns her smile. "Good, then I'm going to make myself clear. I personally don't give a fuck whether you're with Aiden or not. If you need someone for any reason, you can call me, day or night." He gives Aiden a stern look. "I'll be there, and I will hurt anyone that tries to hurt you. I don't care who they are. I promise."

Rebecca can feel herself choking up. No one has ever cared that much for her before – at least they've never voiced it. She can also tell Max's words are not sitting well with Aiden right now. "Aww, Max. That's one of the sweetest things anyone has ever said to me. Thank you." She clinks her glass to his and swallows her shot, placing her glass back on the table. "I desperately need to pee before I add

any more liquid to this body. Excuse me a minute."
What I really need to do is remove myself from this conversation. Aiden looks edgy, and Max seems to be ticked off at something. What better way to escape than a bathroom run. Men never question those.

As she's closing the bathroom door, she overhears Max talking to Aiden in an angry tone.
"Aiden, don't be a fucking dick. Just give her to me. I'll treat her right for the right reasons." Max sounds more pissed with each word he speaks.

Aiden chuckles. "You're just pissed I tried to exclude you. I have no intention of hurting her or letting you have her, Max. Rebecca and I have some things to discuss when the times right."

Max swallows his shot and slams his glass down on the table. "Come on, bro. I saw the fucking contract. You're hoarding her for 30 days like a greedy little child, then you're going to set her free. That is one of the stupidest things you could ever do. I mean, have you been paying attention? She's not in this for the money. She truly wants to be here. Have you even discussed our original plan with her?" Aiden takes a deep breath and leans back in his seat. "Yeah, that's what I thought. Well, then you better make your move, or I will. Destroy that contract and put a ring on that girl. If you don't, I gladly will."

Wait, what original plan? And, I'm sorry, but did Max just say he'd marry me?
Rebecca clears her throat and shuts the door harder than necessary to let them know she's coming. "Hey! Do either of you know how to make slippery nipples?"

Both men instantly spin their heads toward her with their eyes wide. She swears as though Aiden just gulped when Max suddenly bursts out laughing. "Fuck, princess. My heart stopped for a minute!" He slaps Aiden on the back. "Relax, old man. It's a fucking shooter. She stunned me for a minute too."

Oh, shit! Whoops!

Giggling, she snuggles up to Aiden. "I'm sorry. I just realized how that must have sounded. Max is right. It's a shooter. I think it's Bailey's and Sambuca."

Max ducks behind the bar and starts sorting through bottles of alcohol. "You got it, babe." He slams a bottle of Sambuca and a bottle of Bailey's Irish cream down on the bar. "I'll give you a slippery nipple, or anything else you can think of for that matter. Just say the word."

Rebecca can see Aiden's nostrils flare when he glares at Max. "Okay! I don't want to hear you say you're going to give her a slippery nipple. I am certainly not a prude. I know it's a drink, but Jesus, Max, I know what you're suggesting, and you're coming on a bit too strong!"

Rebecca kisses his cheek. "Baby, he's just trying to get you going."

Max sits three shot glasses on the table and bellows as he raises his glass. "To the nipples, I intend to make slippery in the next three weeks! And I'm not talking about drinks!" He clinks his glass with theirs.

Aiden stares at Rebecca with a wicked smile. "I have no problem making your nipples slippery."

"Oh, for goodness sake! It's just a damn drink! You two are

such men!" Rebecca downs her drink and slaps her glass on the table for effect.

Laughing, Max winks. "I'd say one more of these, and you should be just about ready for an orgasm."

She bursts out laughing as Aiden's face turns red. He picks up a magazine from the rack alongside the table and heaves it at Max's head. "I'm not fucking with you, Max! That's enough!"

Grabbing Aiden's arm, she tries to control her laughter as she wipes the tears from her cheeks. "Aiden, you let him get to you so easily. It's just another shooter." She laughs. Aiden looks skeptical, but he doesn't often frequent bars. "I'm serious. It really is a shooter. They're Kahlua, Amaretto and Bailey's." She looks over at Max for confirmation. "Right?"

Max laughs as he nods. "Yeah, you're right, but you should have let him stew on that one a bit." He chucks his chin in Aiden's direction. "I know I'm gonna." Wiping his hands with a damp towel, he winks at Rebecca and smiles. "Anyway, I'm going to go check on dinner. I don't know about you two, but I'm getting kinda hungry."

Crossing his arms, Aiden watches Max stroll into the kitchenette. Once out of sight, Aiden turns his attention back to Rebecca. Lifting her chin with his finger, he raises his brow. "You thought that was funny, huh?"

Smiling, Rebecca tips her head into her shrug. "Oh, come on, Aiden. He's just toying with you."

Taking her hand, he kisses her, gently pulling her from her seat. "Mmhmm, I'm not so convinced that he is, but

I'm not going to let him bother me right now. I have much sweeter things on my mind. Why don't I take you to the bedroom so I can show you what I put into an orgasm?"

"Ohh, I think you've shown me this before, but I'm always open to experiencing it again," she giggles.

"I hope so because I'd like to try something a little different this time." He flicks on the light and reaches into the bag by the door. Rebecca's about to dart for the bed when Aiden grabs her arm. "Not so fast." Dangling a blindfold from his finger, he winks. "What do you say we check something else off that list?"

Biting her lip, Rebecca stares at the black piece of silk swaying in his hand. "A blindfold?"

Smiling, he waggles his eyebrows. "Don't look so shocked. Many couples use blindfolds. Now, turn around and let me do it up for you."

She turns slowly, her heart racing as the smooth fabric covers her eyes. "Aiden—"

His warm breath ruffles her hair with a quiet *"shhh"* before placing a light kiss next to her ear. "Relax, baby. I only have pleasure in mind."

Nodding, she rolls her head and takes a deep breath. "You know, on second thought, obviously this plane is much smaller than your place, and I'm almost certain it's not soundproof either. Maybe we shouldn't. I mean, what if Max hears us? I don't feel like enduring any more taunting."

Chuckling, Aiden guides her to a stool in the middle of the room and lightly presses her shoulders, guiding her down. "I really don't care if he does, but if it bothers you" – he kisses the top of her head – "the TV should take care of that. Now, I think you're just nervous about the blindfold, and I promise you have no reason to be. Trust me, Rebecca, you're going to enjoy this."

The television comes to life, and Rebecca's head turns, then quickly turns again to the sound of shuffling somewhere close. The faint smell of Aiden's cologne lingers next to her, but she can't decipher where he's gone. Then the soft touch of his fingers lightly trail down her spine. "Relax, baby, I'm here. The blindfold is only meant to heighten your senses, not to trick you. I want you to focus on your body – my touch."

His deep voice is soothing as his hand caresses the length of her side, and she arches into his touch. Her head rolls to her shoulder, a muffled *'Mmm'* leaving her lips as she seeks him out. Just then, the feathery breeze of his warm breath drifts across her exposed neck, pushing goosebumps to the surface of her flesh. Her breath catches, and she moistens her lips, her mouth suddenly as dry as the desert.

The back of his hand gently glides along her jawbone, his thumb tracing the edge of her bottom lip as she lifts her chin. The soft lips that meet hers feel almost foreign. The lack of sight making him a stranger but one that knows her desires all too well.

His hand slides behind her neck as he deepens their kiss, and at the first hint of his tongue, she's already wet. As the moist warmth of his lips move over hers, she reaches out to touch him – to feel this new mystery man bringing her senses to life. He smiles against her lips, folding his fingers over hers. A warm breath flutters across her ear as he whispers, "No touching, Rebecca."

The contact disappears, and her muscles tense. He has her waiting for his touch, needing so badly to feel his hands once again. Her mind whirls with thoughts of the final page of their contract. The things she once feared, now making her clit sing. She wiggles in her seat, wanting desperately to tear off the blindfold. It's Aiden – she knows that, but she needs to see him – the one that's stirring these carnal desires she thought she kept so deep.

She inhales sharply as his muscular arms surround her—his arousal clearly defined as it presses against her back. He grasps her knees, gently easing them apart as his voice rumbles, "I want you, Rebecca." His hand glides along her inner thigh, smoothing over the damp crease of her panties, then slips inside. "I want to feel you come apart in my hands."

Be it his provocative words, his intoxicating cologne or the lack of sight, he's sparked desperation like she's never felt. Inhaling, she leans back, a breathy *"Oh yes"* seeping through her lips as she exhales. She lifts her bottom and grabs his wrist, thrusting his fingers inside. "Christ yes, Rebecca," he growls, rocking his palm against her mons.

Determined to end this incredible ache he's created, she presses her cheek to his bicep and rocks hard against his hand. Her breaths quicken as her legs and lips spread, and a euphoric *"Ohh"* surges from her chest.

"That's it baby, cum for me."

"Oh god yes," she gasps. Her legs trembling as every muscle in her body strains. She's never felt so wanton, never acted so untamed. Heat rakes her body, and for the first time tonight, she doesn't want to take the blindfold off.

Aiden unties the black silk from around her eyes, and she tucks her chin to her chest. "Don't shy away from me, Rebecca." He grabs her hand, placing it on his bulging groin. "Do you feel that? I've never been so turned on by a display." The corner of her mouth tightens, and he slides his finger under her chin, lifting it to kiss her. "It mystifies me how you affect me."

A shy smile graces her face as she shrugs. "I feel like I should apologize."

Throwing his head back, Aiden laughs. "Absolutely not."

Rebecca sits up, her eyes narrowing. "But you didn't" – she points to his groin – "you know, cum," she says, searching his face. He shrugs, and she takes his hand. "Come to the bed. I want to try something."

"Try something, huh. You mean you've never—" Aiden's words trail off as she shakes her head and shoves him onto the bed. "Baby, you don't —"

Tugging down his briefs, she peers up from between his legs. "Shhh, just let me try. I promise if you don't like it, I'll stop."

Laughing, Aiden lets his head fall back to the bed. "Oh, I can assure you that won't be an issue."

Rebecca wraps her hand around the base, cupping his balls in her other palm and licks her lips. She's confident about this move because she recalls seeing it in one of those dirty movies her father used to hide in their garage.

She might not have watched the entire act, but surely this isn't rocket science.

She licks off the droplet of pre-cum and wets her lips, closing her mouth over the head. A deep moan rises from Aiden's chest as he watches his shaft disappear.

His flesh is so soft that she feels the need to explore every tiny ridge, rolling her tongue along his length. Slowly working her way down, she's surprised when he hits the back of her throat with still a fist full before the base. Swallowing, he gains passage, and for the tiniest of moments, Rebecca wonders what it would be like if he came now. She hears Aiden groan *"Ah god"* above her and peers up. He's gripping the sheets in one hand as the other flies to the back of her head. "Fuck, baby, if you don't stop, I'm going to cum."

Slowly releasing him from her throat, she gives him approval. "Then do it. I want you to, Aiden. I want to taste you."

"Holy christ, Rebecca," he exhales, falling back to the bed.

She runs her tongue along the large muscle underneath, circles the rim of his head then sinks her mouth back over his shaft. Aiden's hips begin to lift and lower, pushing himself deeper into her throat with each stroke. His hand slides through her hair, coming to rest on the back of her head as his hips jolt. "Ahhh—fuck." As the warm salty liquid hits the back of her throat, she thinks, *Hmm, it's very much like salty raw eggs.* Swallowing, she holds him in her mouth and places her hand on his chest, wondering if the pulse between her lips matches his heartbeat. *How silly is that question, I wonder?*

Aiden takes a deep breath and slides his hands under her arms. "Come up here." He wraps his arms around her, his kiss almost as intense as his release. "My god, Rebecca. I thought you said you had never done that before."

Laughing nervously, she shrugs. "I haven't. Only right here. Why? That must be a good thing then, right? Was it okay?"

Blowing out through partially pursed lips, he kisses her forehead. "Are you kidding? Yes, it was okay. Hell, I might even say that was exceptionally okay," he chuckles, pulling her against his chest with a growl. Then, taking another deep breath, he strokes her hair. "God, I could lie here all day, but I suppose we should go get cleaned up for dinner."

After their shower, she pulls on a clean skirt and tank top then heads out to the main cabin. As she feared, Max is watching a movie. He smiles up at her, and she waits for his taunting, but not this time. This time Max seems different. His smile is sweet, almost understanding when he says, "I'm sorry I ever joked with you that day. I thought" – he throws his hands up – "well, I'm sure you know what I mean. Chicks don't usually stick around for longer than a day." He shifts his weight and smiles, looking almost uncomfortable himself. "Don't be embarrassed, princess. It's completely natural." He switches off the TV and winks. "Now that I've cleared that up, you should know that I'm free to go back to razzing you." A big grin settles on his face as he sets the remote down. "Dinner's done. Danielle was just waiting on you two." He gives her a chaste kiss on the cheek. "I'll let her know you're ready."

Aiden walks over to the dining table, laces his hand through her hair and pulls her head back for a kiss. *It's a completely savage kiss, one that makes me want to take him right back to that bedroom and one that's so out of character for the almighty Aiden Collins. I fucking love it!*

"Thanks." He runs his hand down the side of her face. "I should've said that before you left the room. I apologize." Smiling, she remembers the look on his face as he gripped the sheets. That was all the thanks she required.

Max flops down across from them with a grin. "So, what were you two doing in there," he asks, waggling his eyebrows at Aiden.

Taking a drink, a smirk forms on Aiden's face. "Well, we were just working on one of those crazy named drinks. Tell me, Max, is there one called the satisfied clit?"

Biting the inside of his cheek, Max nods as Rebecca's cheeks redden.

Chapter 8 – Jamaica

Dinner looks amazing, consisting of prime rib with gravy, roasted potatoes, and baby carrots. Max opens a large bottle of red wine and pours them each a glass. The guys seem unusually quiet during dinner, so Rebecca decides to open a neutral conversation. "What time will it be when we arrive?"

"I think Andre said we'd be arriving around 9 pm, Jamaica time. We'll still have time to hit the bar," Max winks. "In fact," he says, dropping his fork with a big smile. He wipes his mouth, pulling out his travel envelope from his bookbag beside his seat and hands it to Rebecca. "I booked myself in the presidential suite. It's perfect for after-hour parties. Oh, and you two are booked into the master swim out. You have your own hot tub and pool." Refilling their wine glasses, he settles back in his chair and smiles. "We can party all night if your little heart desires, princess. My room never closes."

Aiden closes his eyes, shaking his head. "Perfect. This is going to be three weeks of partying for you two, isn't it?" He studies Rebecca's face watching the slight smile tug at her lips as she takes a sip of her wine.
God, Max is right. She is everything we've been searching for. She's sweet, innocent when necessary, but still wild, crazy and adventurous. I just don't think I can bring myself to

share her.

Max clinks his glass with Rebecca's. "Abso-fucking-lutely, bro! Join in or back the fuck off! No buzzkills allowed. Right, Becca?"

Smiling, Rebecca nods. "I have to agree, Aiden. You have zero worries here. No one knows you. When we leave here in three weeks, we'll never have to see any of them ever again." She stands and raises her glass in the air. "Try that crazy-named drink, Aiden. Hell, just eat that fucking hotdog!"

Aiden and Rebecca burst out laughing while Max sits back and stares, obviously not understanding her last statement. Though he does raise a brow when Aiden raises his glass and gives a curt nod. "You're right. We're here on vacation. I'll try to loosen up a little, but someone still needs to be the voice of reason. After all, someone has to make sure you two don't get yourselves into trouble."

Max laughs. "We're going to be at an all-inclusive adults-only resort. How can we possibly get into trouble? The only thing you need to do, little brother, is lighten the fuck up."

Aiden squeezes Rebecca's hand and smiles. "Don't worry. We're going to have a good time." Finishing off his wine, he stands. "Excuse me, I'll be right back. Too much wine," he winks.

Andre announces they'll be landing a half-hour earlier than expected, getting them into Montego Bay at 8:30 pm. Max and Rebecca cheer, startling Aiden as he opens the bathroom door. Throwing his arm out with a smile, he draws it back to his rib cage and bows. "Well, thank you.

I've been doing it all by myself since I was about two. It's really not that big of a deal anymore."

Laughing, Rebecca holds her hand out. "Come here, silly. We weren't cheering about your peeing skills. We're going to be arriving early – we're almost there."

Max chuckles, patting him on the back. "But I bet your peeing skills are pretty boss too, bro."

A limo is waiting at the airport to take them to the resort when they land. Their chauffeur, a tall, dark Jamaican gentleman with a slender frame, is wearing a suit that is at least two sizes too big. He's standing next to the car with a ceaseless smile, and regardless of what they say to him, his response remains the same, "Oh yes, no worries."

Only one phrase differs. When he opens the back door to the limo and hands Max a joint, his ceaseless smile still in place, he says, "Welcome to Jamaica, Sir. Compliments of the resort."

Rolling his eyes, Aiden shakes his head. "Oh, that's real classy, Max. What kind of resort is this again?"

Laughing, Max holds his hands up in defence. "It's not like I ordered it, Aiden. This is Jamaica. Maybe it's how they greet all their guests. It is an adults-only resort, that just means no one under the age of twenty-one. Nothing else." He nudges Rebecca. "That makes you just barely legal here, little one."

"Sounds like more reason for me to celebrate," she smiles.

Pulling her into his side, Aiden chuckles. "Jesus, Max. What are you doing to her?"

As soon as the limo starts moving, Max lights the joint. He takes a couple of drags and hands it to Rebecca. She's never smoked weed before, but when in Jamaica...

She glances over at Aiden as he shrugs and shakes his head, then takes a drag, nearly choking half to death. He rubs her back, trying to stifle his laughter while Max breaks out into a full roar. "Damn, princess. You've got a halo hanging somewhere, huh? Here" – he passes it back to her – "take small pulls."

Holding it to her lips, she takes a small puff, and Max places his finger over her lips before she can exhale. "There. Now, hold it in."

When she finally exhales, her head spins for a brief second, and she's not sure if it's from lack of oxygen or the weed. She blinks several times, trying to refocus, and Max passes it back to her. "Again. Just go easy. Remember, little puffs."

Inhaling, she holds it without being prompted this time and passes it back to Max.

Grinning, he reaches for the joint. "Ah, you're a quick learner."

When she exhales, she can feel the high making its presence known.
Oh my god.
She holds out her hand and pinches her arm.
Shit. I am sooo high.
Her hand flies to her mouth, her eyes wildly searching Max and Aiden's face.
Did I just say that out loud?

She drops her hand and rests back in her seat with a chuckle.

Pfft, it doesn't matter. But, wait, am I laughing in my head, or can they hear me?

She cups her hand over her lips, pinching them together.

My lips feel like they're being held hostage in a huge grin. Hehe, that's silly, but it was kind of funny. Damn, did I eat dirt?

Max looks at her, pointing as his head falls back with laughter. "Shit, princess! You're so stoned! You should see your perma-grin!"

Max's laughter sets her off on her own laughing journey, and she peers over at Aiden, trying to focus through her tears. The hope that his serious face will help settle her giggles is lost when he starts to laugh. "Wow, baby, he's right. There is no denying you're high."

When they arrive at the resort, they're an absolute laughing mess. Their driver opens the limo door, releasing a puff of smoke you'd only see in a bad Cheech and Chong movie. Aiden steps out through the curls of smoke, watching as the two of them try desperately to contain their laughter and remain on their feet. He holds his hand out to Max. "Give me the itinerary. I think I should check us in."

Still laughing, Max reaches into his pocket, pulling out the paperwork for their reservations, and hands them to Aiden. "Yeah, good idea, bro."

Chuckling, Aiden slaps Max on the back and takes the papers from his hands. "Yeah."

As he hands the itinerary to the gentleman so the concierge can prepare their rooms, Max leans his big body against a statue. A loud *"Oh Shit"* booms through the main entrance as the sculpture crashes to the ground. He bends over, trying to pick up the pieces as staff members rush over to help. "Fuck! I'm really sorry, man," his laughter breaking through his words.

Rebecca is rolling with laughter while Aiden tries to explain that they don't usually smoke weed but indulged at the driver's urging. Thankfully, the concierge has obviously dealt with this kind of thing before. He raises his hands with a smile and nods. "No worries, Sir. Let's get you to your rooms, and we'll take care of everything."

Another gentleman graciously waves them forward. "Collins party?" Aiden puts his hand up, confirming with a nod. "Welcome to Montego Bay! My name is Devon. If you follow me, please, I'll show you to your rooms."

Max holds up his hand with an odd look. "Uh, dude. What about our bags?"

"Yes, Sir. They're already in your rooms. Please, follow me." Turning, he waves them forward.

Max's brows shoot up as he grabs Aiden's arm. "Holy shit! He didn't say no worries!"

Rebecca is still trying to recover from the statue incident when she bursts into laughter once again. Smacking him on the back, Aiden tries his best not to give a reaction. "I think that was all for entertainment. What do you say we just follow him to our rooms, huh?"

Weaving their way through the resort to the backside by the open coves, the gentleman stops and opens the first door to a large, beautifully decorated suite. He turns around, his eyes questioning between Max and Aiden. "Mr. Maxwell Collins. The Presidential Suite, Sir."

Max takes the key card from his hand and salutes. "Thanks, kind sir." He stuffs a $50 bill in his pocket and places his finger to his lips. "Shhh. I won't tell if you don't. It's not fair that they don't allow you guys to accept tips." He walks inside with his arms outstretched and hollers, "Woohoo! You two come get me once you get settled in!"

Rebecca and Aiden follow the gentleman a little further down the path to the next door. He slides the key card through the lock and holds out his arm. "Here you are, Mr. & Mrs. Aiden Collins. The Master Swim Out Suite."

Aiden's brow lifts. He knows it's likely an assumption on the concierge's behalf, but he actually likes the sound of it. He peers over at a questioning Rebecca with a smirk and takes the key. "Thank you."

As soon as the door closes, Rebecca shifts her weight to one hip and tilts her head with a sideways smile. "So, I'm Mrs. Collins here, am I?"

Smiling, he wraps his arms around her waist. "I'm sure it was a simple assumption. Although it does have a nice ring to it, don't you think?" He kisses the top of her head and takes her hand. "Shall we check this place out?"

Though the concierge called it a room, it's really more of a villa, with an airy and inviting open concept. There is a small kitchenette immediately to your right as you walk into the suite that houses a microwave and refrigerator, along with a couple of other small appliances. The living room is large, with finished concrete flooring that you'd swear is marble. All walls are white, with the exception of one. An accent wall on the left is tiled in black glass and has a built-in flat screen and a full-length ribbon fireplace. A black leather sectional faces the floor-to-ceiling window doors that retract into the wall to reveal a step-in hot tub and swim-up pool. And just beyond the fireplace wall is a king-size bedroom with a double soaker tub set into the corner window. The bathroom is done in multi-tone grey stone and has an oversized shower with a waterfall head and a separate room for the toilet.

Rebecca is lost in amazement. She knows this suite must have cost a small fortune when even Aiden wraps his arms around her and takes a deep breath. "Well, it looks like Max has really outdone himself."

She scans the massive living area and nods. "I'd say. I've never seen anything like this." She grabs his arm. "Oh my god! We have to go see his room. He has the presidential suite, and he said it has a party room."

Shaking his head, Aiden groans. "God, what *has* he done to you?"

Dragging him along reluctantly, they head for the door – she must see Max's room. Knocking, Aiden opens the door and walks in. The decor is the same, except his suite is twice the size, occupying two full floors. There's a balcony off the living room upstairs that overlooks the ocean and, of course, Aiden and Rebecca's pool. There's a dance floor beside a small bar area on the lower level, fully equipped with a disco ball and spotlights. Prominent column speakers stand in every corner and run all the way up to the second floor for the sound system. Rebecca grasps Aiden's arm. "He wasn't kidding. This really is a party room."

Max hollers from down the hall. "Hey! Come check this shit out!"

Following his voice, they find him in his bedroom. It's twice the size of theirs, with a king-size bed and a walk-out terrace that overlooks their hot tub. The bed nestles against the wall at one end of the room, while at the far end, he has a hot tub and a minibar. Rebecca's mouth drops open. "This is freaking amazing! How did you find this place?"

He shrugs, leading them back out to the rest of the unit. "I researched the best adult-only resorts in Jamaica." He fans his arms out. "This was rated the best in Montego. So, I booked it."

Aiden pats his back. "You really have outdone yourself, brother. Great choice."

"It was an opportunity that I couldn't pass up," Max winks. Disappearing into his room, he comes out in a fresh pair of black shorts and a white t-shirt and claps his hands. "All right. Let's go check out the bar."

They follow the path and the music leading to the bar. Rebecca can see Aiden is finally loosening up as they dance along the pathway to the music. As they get closer, the music gets louder, and all at once, they face each other, simultaneously yelling out, "One Love!"

Rebecca grabs hold of Aiden and Max, pulling them along excitedly. "Oh my god, I love Bob Marley!"

Aiden laughs, trying to keep up with her. "Baby, I think you still love everything right now. I'm not sure I've ever seen anyone so high."

Walking into the central pavilion, they see a few people dancing, and there's a couple at the bar. Still, it's certainly not as active as they expected. When they approach the bartender, Max asks where everyone is. The gentleman smiles, and in a thick Jamaican accent, says, "At di beach fa di welcome tradition." He points toward the beach. "Yuh muss guh or it be bad luck, yuh know." He hands them each a towel, shooing them off. "Guh, yuh muss guh now."

Max turns to face Rebecca and Aiden, rubbing his hands together. "Well, we don't want any bad luck now, do we. Let's go!" Taking Rebecca's hand, Aiden follows Max toward the beach. As they approach, they spot a bunch of nude bodies dancing near the waterfront with a low-lying cloud of smoke lingering just above. From the overpowering smell of weed wafting through the air, the chances of it being from the small bonfire are slim to none.

Clearing his throat, Aiden halts Rebecca. "I don't think this is the right place."

Grabbing his arm, Max tugs him forward with a stern look. "Yeah, I'm pretty sure it is. Let's ask someone." He heads over to a naked lady, dancing by herself and tries to get her attention. "Excuse me, darling. Is this the welcoming ritual?"

Running her hands down his face while she dances in place, she gives him a toothy smile. "Yep, it is. Damn, you're a handsome one, aren't you?" Giggling, she reaches for his shirt. "But you have way too many clothes on, honey. Let me help you."

Aiden's eyes grow wide. "Well, this is a different type of welcome than I had expected."

She spins, her eyes locking onto him with a moan. "Ohh, am I seeing double again? Here honey, let me help you get undressed."

Backing up, Aiden puts his hands out in front of him. "No no, I'm fine. I believe we're in the wrong place."

Staring at Aiden and Rebecca, Max takes off his shirt in his usual devil-may-care manner. "Fuck it! What can it hurt? Everyone else is naked. Come on, take it off. It's dark, and we're going in the water anyway."

Aiden eyes Rebecca with a stern look. "Don't you dare, Rebecca."

She snickers, toying with the hem of her tank top. "Come on, Aiden, it's a tradition. I don't want bad luck while we're here." Her eyes plead with his as she pulls her tank top over her head, tossing it at him with a giggle.

"Woo! That a girl, Becca," Max cheers.

"Rebecca." Aiden's voice drips with warning.

Max laughs. "Come on, bro. Pull the stick out of your ass and take your clothes off."

Reaching for the clasp on her bra, she joins in Max's coaxing. "Come on, baby. I'm afraid to touch the bottom. I need you to carry me into the water unless, of course, you want Max to carry me in."

A mischievous grin forms on Max's face as he stares over

at Aiden. "No problem, princess. I'll gladly carry you in."

"Like fuck, you will," Aiden bellows, stripping off his shirt and tossing it at Max's head. "You knew this was a thing, didn't you, Max?"

Max shakes his head, laughing at Aiden's response. "Nah, bro, really, but I think it's fucking great. It's like getting a fucking detailed menu."

Aiden drops his shorts, watching Rebecca pull off her skirt and panties, gritting his teeth. "Yeah, fucking great."

Max whistles and chucks his chin at Aiden. "Holy fuck! You definitely found a keeper, bro." Smiling, he darts for the water.

Lifting Rebecca into his arms, Aiden strides for the ocean. "Jesus Rebecca, you could drive a man insane." Cradling her close to his chest, he dunks them into the warm Caribbean water, staying only long enough to ensure they've gotten wet. He tosses her over his shoulder, her bottom in the air as he walks back into shore to get dressed.

Dangling down his back, she smacks his backside in protest. "Aiden! Put me down. We're onshore."

Putting his hand out as he runs by, Max slaps Rebecca's butt. She yelps, reaching back to put her hands over her bottom with a chuckle. "Damn it, Max!"
Damn is right! I'm not sure I ever found a swap to my bottom arousing before.

"Let the games begin, little one!" He watches the glow of his handprint appear across her cheek and smiles.
Fucking perfect.

As Rebecca is slipping her skirt on, she peers up, catching a glimpse of Max's naked glory. Taking a moment to appreciate the perfect male form before her, she allows her eyes to travel from his muscular calves all the way to his eyes – the very same eyes that are staring back into hers. Smiling slyly, he fastens his shorts. "I'm gonna go scope out the bar. Are you two coming or what?"

Rebecca's shocked when Aiden nods. "Yeah, I guess we may as well. We just bared ourselves to all these people. I'd say we're kinda like family now."

The bar still isn't packed, but there are definitely more patrons present than before. Saddling up alongside the bar, Max pats the stool beside him. "Come on, princess, have a seat." He waves his hand at the bartender and holds three fingers in the air. "Three Bob Marley shots, a gin and tonic and two Jamaican rums straight up, please."

The bartender smiles with a wave, signifying he's heard him. Aiden stands next to Rebecca with his arm wrapped around her waist and places his lips to her ear. "We'll just have a couple of drinks, and then we'll go back to our room."

"That sounds good to me," she nods with a smile, letting images of their first night together in his pool dance around her mind.

The bartender delivers their drinks, and Max raises his glass high. "Cheers! To the three of us, may we spend our vacation wasted and have a shit ton of new adventures in Jamaica!"

"Woo!" Rebecca hollers, clanking her glass with his and

Aiden's. She slides her empty glass back to Max. "Another!"

Aiden's hand tightens around her waist, and she hears Max holler. "Yeah! That's my girl!" He waves at the bartender. "We'll have another round of Marley shooters, boss!"

Before Max can lower his arm, a sexy dark-skinned beauty locks her arm around his and plants herself on the stool next to him. "Hey, honey. Are you looking for a good time?"

He glares over at her in disgust and laughs. "Sugar, I'm having a good time, and it's already paid for. Now get your dirty paw off me before I call over the resort security."

"Well, you definitely aren't as friendly as you look, are you," she huffs.

"Yeah? How's this for friendly? Fuck off, bush pig!" He shoots her a disgusted look, spinning back to face Rebecca and Aiden.

"That was a bit harsh, Max. I thought you wanted to find women," Rebecca says.

He shakes his head. "Princess, you have no idea what you're talking about. That was not a woman. That was a prostitute. I will never be that desperate. Besides, I already have my eye on a woman."

Aiden kisses Rebecca's cheek. "Drink your shot, baby, and let's go dance."

Tipping back her shot, she pats Max on the arm. "I'm sorry, Max. Good call. You definitely don't want to take home any dirty pussy." Winking at him, she slides into Aiden's arms.

"Cute, princess. Real cute!" Max slugs back his rum and motions to the bartender for another.

They head out to the dance floor as Zayn croons Pillowtalk. Rebecca lifts her arms, slowly lowering them over Aiden's head. Their kiss is tender as he runs his hands down her sides to her hips. Her hands slide down his chest, caressing his pecs, then suddenly, he spins her around. Pulling her into him, he presses his groin against her backside and rolls his hips into her bottom. She reaches back, grasping the nape of his neck and whines her body with his. "Mmm, I love the way you dance. I would never have guessed you could move like you do," she says, laying her head back against his shoulder to savour his delicate touch.

His lips brush against her collarbone, laying a light kiss on her neck. "There's a lot you don't know about me, Rebecca."

"I'm sure there is." Her eyes flutter closed, letting the music move their bodies. When the song fades to the classic Bump and Grind by R. Kelly, she feels a second hard body form against her. A leg presses between her thighs, she lifts her head, her eyes springing open to Max. He's nestled firmly against her, looking down at her with an alluring smile. "Max?"

Aiden's chest shakes against her back as he laughs. "Relax, baby. It's a dance. You can't tell me you've never done the bump and grind before."

Holy shit! Is that a drummer playing between my thighs?

Having these two grind their groins simultaneously into me is shrouding my thoughts. Okay, I should stop Max — but it feels so damn good.

Her head falls back to Aiden's chest as she rolls her eyes. *And my hips chose now to have a mind of their own.*

"Of course, I have, Aiden, but you did say not to encourage Max," she says, her mind bathing in alcohol and a touch of ecstasy.

She gasps as the heat of Max's tongue sears the flesh between her breasts, working across her collarbone to her neck. His soft lips brush against her ear. "Trust me, princess. He didn't mean what he said."

And the drummer just picked up his pace, playing a master's solo between my thighs.

Aiden cups her breasts, breathing heavily into her hair. "Shhh, you can relax, baby. I've seen the way you've been looking at him. Besides, you told me to loosen up and honestly, we're just dancing."

Oh my god! Is this really happening right now?

The song comes to an end, and Max slowly backs away, his eyes remaining on hers. He takes her hand and presses it to his lips with a low growl. "Thanks for the dance, princess." His stare meets Aiden's. "You need to change your mind before I stop being so fucking brotherly." Kissing Rebecca on the cheek, he heads back to the bar.

Turning to face Aiden, Rebecca wraps her arms around his neck and raises her brow. "Change your mind about what?"

"Meh, he's been drinking." He pats her bottom and turns

her toward the bar. "Let's go have a drink."

Rebecca takes her seat beside Max, and he slides a shooter in front of her, nudging her elbow with his. "Drink up, Princess. There's another round coming."

Sitting down next to her, Aiden seems to be miles away as he sips his rum. Max slides another set of shooters down to them and holds his in the air with a grin. "To dirty dancing. May there be much more where that came from." He winks, downing his shooter and slams his glass down on the bar. "And, on that note. I'm gonna call it a night before I start some shit. I'll see you two kids in the morning."

Rebecca turns as Max leans over to kiss her cheek, catching the corner of her mouth. His eyes flick to hers, and she quickly looks away. "Goodnight, Max."

He knocks Aiden's fist and points. "Goodnight, bro. Tomorrow for sure."

The corner of Aiden's mouth turns down as he chucks his chin. "We'll see." He looks at Rebecca, holding up his empty glass. "You ready to call it a night, baby?"

"I'm ready to go back to our room," she says, sliding onto his lap as she runs her tongue across his lips.

"Mmm, now that, I like to hear." Grabbing hold of her waist, he tosses her over his shoulder like a sack of potatoes. Her hands slapping off his back in protest as she giggles.

Tossing her onto the bed, Aiden hovers over her. His cobalt eyes looking deep into hers as he slides his hand up her skirt. "Tisk tisk. Did you leave your panties at the beach?" She nods with a chuckle. "No wonder you were so worked up while we were dancing tonight."

"In my defence, they were full of sand, and how was I to know I would be sandwiched between two of the hottest twin brothers I've ever met. Besides, I told you I hate clothes, remember?"

Tugging off her skirt, he tosses it to the floor with a chuckle. "That you did, baby. That you did." He flops down beside her, his grin slowly fading as his hand trails along her stomach. His fingers briefly toying with the hem of her tank top before pushing it over her breasts.

The light touch of his fingertips tickle, and she jolts upward with a giggle. Grabbing his hand, she pulls him over. "Aiden, stop teasing me."

Gently pushing her back to the bed, Aiden kisses her, "I like teasing you." He slides down, circling her nipple with his tongue, then sucks it into his mouth and releases it, making a loud popping noise. She giggles, dropping her hand to the back of his head as he moves down her body with a moan. "God, I've wanted to do this all night."

As he slides between her legs, Aiden lets out a growl, pushing her knees to her chest as he buries his face. Her back arches, an erotic *"Ah yes"* coming from her parted lips as she grasps the pillow. His tongue slides through her folds, delving deep into her opening, and she clutches the fabric so tight in her hands she can feel her fingertips burn.

The only thing she can think of at this very moment is the sensation rapidly blooming from her core. A feral moan resonates around her, and she squeezes her eyes, pushing her face closer to the pillow. *Oh my god, that's not me.* But when Aiden pulls her swollen bud between his lips and sucks. There's no question – it's her making that sound.

Waves of excitement wash over her, tensing her muscles from the inside out. Her thighs shake as she pushes them against Aiden's hands. "Oh – My — God," she cries out, shoving at his head.

He releases her legs and peers up with a smile. "God, I love the sound of you giving over. Why don't you let me show you how good I can grind now that we're alone."

Alcohol and exhaustion are slowly taking over as she sprawls open with a slight moan. "I'm so done."

"Yes, just about, baby." Aiden grabs her bottom, grinding into her as deep as he can. Images float through her mind of the earlier commotion on the dance floor, and she can see herself sandwiched between Max and Aiden. The heat and the lust of the moment completely overpowering her actions.

She peers up at Aiden, a light *"Ah"* leaving her lips as he brings her thoughts soaring back to him. His grip tightens on her bottom, and he plunges, rolling his hips against hers.

Once.

Twice. He slowly grinds into her. "Fuck, you feel so good, Rebecca," he whispers next to her ear.

He thrusts

Once, then again, a slow seductive grind as a throaty *"Ahh"* escapes his lips parted against her cheek.

His head coming to rest on the pillow she was clenching, both completely sated and drained – they fall asleep.

Rebecca wakes the following morning to Aiden withdrawing himself from her body. Her eyelids flutter open to his smiling face. Kissing her forehead, he bounces out of bed. "I'm not sure what happened, but that's a first for me."

"You slept inside me all night," she asks, snickering at the thought of it. Throwing on Aiden's t-shirt, she heads for the bathroom.

Patting her on the bottom as they pass each other, he shrugs. "I suppose I did. I would have taken advantage of that position this morning if Mother Nature didn't insist her call was answered first," he chuckles. "I'm good to go now, though, if you're interested."

Good to his word, Aiden's lying sprawled out naked on his back when she walks out of the bathroom. Giggling, she lies down beside him. "You're ready now, are you? As I recall, you're the one who called me insatiable. Isn't that what you said?"

His smile broadens as his brow lifts. "I don't mind if we share the title."

Running her hand across his chest, she watches his manhood spring to attention. "Oh! Yes, you are ready to go again," she says, climbing over to straddle him. Leaning down to kiss him, she stops and peers behind to the sound of a knock at the door.

"I don't care. Ignore it." Aiden growls, pulling her back down. "It's probably housekeeping. They can come back later."

Their lips meet only to be disturbed by another knock, only louder and accompanied by Max's deep voice. "Stop fucking and open the door!"

Aiden groans as she breaks their kiss and rolls off him with a chuckle. "You better answer him. You know he's only gonna get louder if you don't."

"God damn it! He can be a real pain in the ass." The frustration ripples off him as he pushes himself off the bed with a grunt. Stabbing his legs into a pair of boxers, he heads toward the door.

Max's boisterous voice echoes through their suite as he walks in the door. "Jesus, do you ever get off her, bro?"

Quickly covering her mouth with her hand to stifle her laugh, she can picture Aiden running his hand through his hair with a cocky smirk when he spits back. "Are you seriously asking me that right now? Would you?"

Rebecca slips her bathing suit on and heads for the living area to find Aiden and Max in the middle of some crazy handshake until Max spots her. He chucks his chin and grins. "Morning, princess. Are you going for a swim before breakfast?"

"Yeah. I was hoping it will wake me up."

"Mind if I join you?" Stripping off his shirt with no concern for her response, he tosses it on the sofa and looks back at Aiden. "Why don't you order us some breakfast, bro. I could really use some steak and eggs benny."

Rebecca waves at Aiden from the pool. "Oh, me too! Please, baby."

Diving into the pool, Max swims up next to her and leans against the ledge. "You looked pretty hot last night, rolling your hips between us. I almost think you wanted more."

Feeling herself flush, she looks into the room for Aiden. "Max," she warns.

Reaching out, he rests his hand on her hip. "No, seriously. I mean it, Becca. That was the hottest thing I've seen in a long fucking time." He licks his lips. "I woke up, still tasting the sweat from your cleavage."

Holy shit! Did he really just say that?
She reaches out, putting her hand on his chest to keep him at a distance. "Max, I don't think Aiden would be pleased if he were to walk out here right now."

He tugs on the string of her bikini bottoms, releasing them from her hips with a feigned look of shock. "Shit. What happened? Do you think he'll be pissed now?"

Gritting her teeth, she reaches for her bottoms, but he holds them high above his head, using his 6'4" frame to his full advantage. "Come on, Max! That's not funny!"

"Aw, come on. I saw you naked last night at the beach, remember? You have no reason to cover up now." His eyes drop, looking down into the water and slowly travel back up to meet hers with a crooked grin. "If Aiden is stupid enough to actually let you go, I plan on making it my goal to make you mine." He shakes his head. "Nah, you know what? Fuck it. I don't care if Aiden thinks you're his or not. He hasn't married you yet. That makes you a free woman in my books."

She can hear Aiden's deep voice before he even steps out onto the patio. "Max! What the fuck are you doing?"

Still holding her bikini bottoms in the air, Max turns to

face him with a shit-eating grin. "Oh, Becca lost her bottoms, and I was trying to help her put them back on, but she's being difficult."

Aiden doesn't look overly amused as he folds his arms over his chest. "Why can't I help but think you had something to do with them getting lost in the first place? Just stop being a child and give them back to her."

Keeping them high above his head, Max smiles. "Of course, bro. That's what I've been trying to do." Turning back, he blows her a kiss and winks. "I told her to come to get them." A mischievous grin slides across his face. "Aren't you going to get them, princess?"

Rebecca looks up at Aiden with pleading eyes, but he shakes his head and shrugs. "I just got dressed, baby."

"Are you kidding me? Really, Aiden?" She brazenly raises her brow, shaking her head. "Okay. Fine." Taking one last look at her obstacle, she charges forward, climbing Max's body like a jungle gym. With her bikini bottoms in hand, she feels like she single-handedly won a round of capture the flag.

Both guys look so stunned that neither one seems to be breathing. With an enormous smile on her face, she slides back down Max's chest with her bottoms in hand. "Yes! I'd call that a victory!"

Aiden's jaw drops. Likely from seeing her girlie parts mashed against Max's face.
Good! Maybe he'll do something next time.

She's not honestly sure Max even knows for certain what just happened. He kind of looks confused. Pointing at Aiden, she raises her brow. "Don't look so shocked, Aiden.

You should have gotten them for me." Turning to face Max with her own well-earned shit-eating grin, she says, "And you... You should've been prepared, big talker."

Max's eyes grow wide as his mouth snaps shut, and he swallows. Then, shaking his head, a broad smile slowly forms. "You're so right. I wasn't ready, princess. Any chance I can get a do-over?"

Laughing, Rebecca shakes her head. "Yeah, that's going to be a no, Max!"

Staring at her in awe, Aiden holds his hand out to help her from the pool. "Jesus, baby. You never cease to amaze me."

Tying her bottoms back on, she reaches for Aiden's extended hand. "Seems you may be open to sharing me with Max after all, huh?" She waits for Aiden to deny it, but he doesn't. Instead, he leans down and gently kisses her cheek.

Well, that was a proverbial punch to the gut. That's fine. Good to know — GOOD TO KNOW!

Forcing a smile, she grabs her towel and heads for their room. "How long before breakfast is here? I'm going to get dressed."

"It should be here in about 5 minutes or so," he hollers back from the patio.

Throwing on a pair of Lycra shorts and a dry bikini top, she adds a touch of liner and pulls her hair up into a messy bun. Aiden opens the door and peeks in. "Breakfast is here, beautiful."

"Yeah, I'm coming." Shutting off the TV, she follows him out.

Max holds his fist out. "Fuck, Becca, you rock! The more I replay that whole scenario — the hotter you look on my face."

Laughing, she smacks his fist away. "Max, you didn't even know what hit you."

"Oh, you may have stunned me, but I know exactly what hit me," he says, waggling his brows with a grin.

Aiden throws his hands up. "Okay, that's enough. We all know what happened out there." He points at Max. "Are you done?" His stare moves to Rebecca. "How about you, are you done?" Smiling, she nods. "Good. Then let's eat."

Breakfast is almost finished when Max sits up and sets his fork down. "Oh shit, I almost forgot with the whole Becca sitting on my face ordeal, but we're supposed to be down in the spa at eleven for the total package. We're booked for mud baths, massages, facials, pedicures and hair treatment—four hours of pampering. Doesn't that sound like heaven," he grins across at Rebecca.

Raising his brow, Aiden leans back in his chair with his coffee. "Facials and pedicures?"

Max shoves a slice of bacon into his mouth and licks the grease from his fingers. "Hey! Don't knock it until you try it, bro."

"I think it sounds wonderful. I've never had a mud bath before. After all, it's all about new experiences. Right, Aiden?" Rebecca can't help but throw that in any chance she gets.

Aiden folds his arms, his chest rising and falling with an

inflated breath. Nodding, the corner of his mouth tugs into a smile, and he swipes his hand over his mouth. "Yes, I suppose you're right." He takes a sip of coffee, looking up through his brows. "But, I'm gonna have to draw the line at the makeup and polish."

Max bursts out laughing. "Hey, that's your loss." He checks the clock and slaps his hand down on the table. "You can decide when we get there. We gotta go."

Chapter 9 – Quality Time

This spa has both indoor and outdoor facilities. Being built amongst a palm grove, it's entirely private both inside and out. As they walk in, they notice the palms growing naturally through the thatched roof. While Rebecca and Aiden look around, Max lets the receptionist know he's booked the family package and signs them in.

The receptionist or she could be a masseuse; it's difficult to tell with their nondescript uniforms. It's one of the things Rebecca has noticed since they've arrived. Not one of the workers could be defined from another based on their uniforms at this resort. All the wait staff, housekeeping, the bartenders, and the maintenance crew, even the souvenir shop attendant wear the same uniform. Either way, this young woman rocks her outfit. She's a beautiful dark-skinned lady in her late 20's, and from both men's reactions, you can tell they're hoping she'll be the masseuse.

Within moments she summons them with a bright smile to follow her through the reception area, leading them to the semi-enclosed deck outside. There are three large stone tubs in a row filled with gray mud, each adorned with rolled towels at the end for a pillow. Besides the stream that runs under the wall giving a feeling of superior tranquillity, Rebecca would have to say it's the least appealing room in the entire spa.

The attendant tells them to strip down, giving them each a pair of thin fibre underwear. "Yuh war only dis," she says as she leaves the room.

Rebecca quickly surmises Jamaica to be quite open sexually when the attendant thinks nothing of leaving them all in the same room to change. It doesn't seem to bother Max either. He doesn't skip a beat stripping off his shorts and pulling on the thin piece of fabric to hop into his tub. "Oh yeah! Now, this is heaven." He raises his brow at them. "What are you two waiting for? Get undressed and get in!"

Aiden blocks Rebecca while she slips into the flimsy panties. Glancing over, Max shakes his head. "Princess, I told you I've already seen it. Besides, Jamaica is not a place to be bashful. We're gonna have to work on that tomorrow when we go to the nude beach. You know, a place where clothing is not an option."

Aiden steps into his tub between Rebecca and Max, taking her hand. "She's not as bashful as you may think. In fact, she hates clothing. Isn't that so, Rebecca?"

Closing her eyes, she chuckles, recalling the look on Aiden's face the night she stripped off her dress in his car. "I'm afraid that's true."

Glaring at Aiden, Max shakes his head. "I see, so Aiden just has you paranoid of stripping down around me then." Max purses his lips as he nods. "Good to know it's not you, princess."

He knocks Aiden's fist. "Well played, bro, but I don't think that's gonna work."

Unsure what Max means by that, Rebecca peers over at Aiden, but he's suddenly miles away as he lightly runs his fingers over her hand. *Maybe he's recalling that first night as well.* She leans forward, smiling at the pair of them. "Well, regardless of clothing, I can't help but think of how lucky I am right now. I mean, look at me. I'm sitting here with the two hottest guys at this resort."
Remaining silent, Aiden smiles and squeezes her hand.

"Woo! That's right, princess," Max hollers, lifting his hand in the air as mud unintentionally splatters onto Aiden. Of course, knowing these two, it just might have been intentional.

"You know, I wouldn't be able to tell you two apart if Max got his hair cut and his beard trimmed," she says, pointing out the apparent differences.

"Well, it seems we'll be testing that out. I'm getting a shave and a haircut today before we leave this building," Max says with a wink. "Oh, this is off topic but, I saw a tattoo parlour in the brochure. So, I was thinking that we could all get some ink as a souvenir to remember our trip."

Scooping up a handful of mud, Rebecca rubs it along her arm. "I'll get one! I've always wanted a tattoo."

"A tattoo Rebecca?" Aiden raises his brow. "I'm pretty sure Max is talking about the permanent kind, not a lick and stick."

Glaring at Aiden, she leans forward. "Sign me up, Max. I'll get a tattoo." Snickering, Aiden shakes his head as she sticks her tongue out. "You know, the permanent kind."

"That's my girl," Max howls, sending mud flying in all directions with a clap of his hands. "I'll book us all an appointment tomorrow. If Aiden wants to bitch out, that's on him." He smiles, pointing to the mud splatter. "Sorry bout that."

Wiping her hands with the cloth at the side of her tub, Rebecca glances over at the men. "Oh! I almost forgot. I saw a billboard outside. A cover band is performing Bob Marley and Marvin Gaye in the central pavilion tonight. We should check them out."

As if to prove he wasn't really paying attention, Aiden turns toward her with his brows drawn together. "Baby, they're both dead."

Rebecca stops rubbing the mud on her arm and stares at him. "I know that, silly. I said it's a cover band."

"Fuck yeah! Marvin Gaye? Like, Sexual Healing Marvin Gaye? Oh, shit yeah. Count me in! I'm always on board for some sexual healing." Max stands, swinging his muddy hips as the curtain to their deck opens, and two beautiful ladies stroll through with a tall, dark mountain of a hunk. The women walk toward Aiden and Max, asking them to follow them to the showerheads along the opposite side of the deck.

The tall, dark wonder holds his hand out to Rebecca. "Good afternoon, my lady. My name is Micah. I'll be your masseuse for today. If you come with me, you can rinse off over here before your massage."

The men let out a loud groan as Micah, the dark God of

massage oil, helps Rebecca out of the tub. Max can't help himself, of course. Rebecca swears there are times he has no control over his outbursts. "Hey, Princess. He didn't really mean *come* with him," Max winks. "In other words, no happy endings, okay?"

Aiden swats him in the arm. "Christ, Max. Shut up!"

Smirking, Micah holds up a robe for Rebecca. "I'll follow you to the shower. Once you've rinsed, you can slip this on, and we'll head down to the massage tables." He glances up at Aiden and Max with a smile. "We'll be using the family massage room today. The three of you will remain together. I do hope you'll all be happy with the end results, but I'm afraid it will not be the happy ending you may have implied, Sir."

Rebecca rinses off, then steps into the robe Micah's holding open for her before following him into the massage room. It's dimly lit, with three tables decently spread in the center of the room. The atmosphere is immediately relaxing, with smooth island tunes playing and at least a couple of dozen candles delivering a delightful smell of jasmine into the air.

Aiden and Max are already lying on their cots face down with a sheet draped across their bottoms when Micah gestures to the empty table. "If you could lie face down, please. We'll start with your back. Do you need a hand up?"

She shakes her head, wondering how she'll achieve it without bearing all, but Micah has it under control. Standing behind her with a sheet, he opens her robe and lets it drop to the floor, quickly replacing it with the sheet.

Then, tugging it under her arms, he gathers it in front of her breasts. "Just hold it here and climb up," he says casually, proving he's done this a billion times.

"Thank you." She climbs onto the cot, letting out a moan as Micah's big hands press firmly into her flesh.

Max's voice rumbles from across the room, "Hey, Princess. If you need gentler hands, let me know. I'd be happy to take his place."

Lifting his head, Aiden's eyes narrow. "Will you shut the fuck up, Max."

The massage is glorious, and at some point, Rebecca must have fallen asleep because she wakes to a deep voice, "Rise and shine, sleepyhead. It's time for our pedicures."

Her body snaps up to a sitting position before she's fully conscious, almost smashing her head into Aiden's. "Shit! I can't believe I fell asleep."

Laughing, Aiden pulls up her sheet. "Relax. It's just time to move on to our next appointment. I've even decided to join you two for the pedicures."

"Pfft, well, of course, you have. Why don't you tell her why bro?" Max takes a deep breath, shifting his weight as he curls his lip. "You don't trust me to be alone with your woman."

"Yes, well, that may have something to do with it," he confirms, helping Rebecca up with a slight smile.

Heading off to get changed, they dress and meet in the main reception area where the pedicure stations are. The pedicures, like everything else so far today, are simply amazing. When they're finished, the guys choose to wait for Rebecca before heading over to the hair salon. They sit sipping on rum while she has her toes airbrushed with palm trees. Then, with pretty toes and the men satisfied from the rum, they head down the hall for their final stop. Aiden and Rebecca only ask for a light trim while Max directs the stylist to give him the same cut and manicured beard as Aiden.

Hearing Max's request, Aiden chucks his chin. "Getting the big boy haircut, Max?"

Stifling her laugh, Rebecca decides it best to say nothing, but she can't wait to see the final result. They're already challenging to tell apart at a quick glance.

"Yeah, gotta grow up someday, right? Besides, it's been a long time since we've sported the same do."

Heading off with their individual stylists, Rebecca gets her hair washed, trimmed and styled. Next, the cosmetician applies some makeup and lets her choose from a wall of different perfumes. She's pleased with the results. Her skin looks absolutely radiant, and it's incredibly soft. Her hair has been straightened, allowing her natural highlights to shine through as it cascades over her shoulders. Just the way Aiden likes it. Her makeup is light, not overwhelming, as some salons may apply. In fact, the cosmetician has done nothing more than add a tint of colour to highlight her natural tones. Finally, Rebecca is left alone in the back room, allowing her a few minutes to examine her final look on her own. When the woman returns, she hands her a garment bag. "Here, dear. Your boyfriend has asked me to have you wear this."

Rebecca opens the garment bag and finds a gorgeous red silk dress. It has a large oval neckline and diagonal mesh strip that wraps around the entire length of the dress, just missing the vital areas. It's classy, sexy and very daring. A shoebox attached to the garment bag produces a pair of red stilettos. They're not fancy, but they're perfectly matched to the dress. Once she changes, she takes one last look in the mirror. She's shocked at her own appearance.

When she opens the door to the main reception, Rebecca's facing true identical twins. She has absolutely no idea which one is Aiden. They're wearing matching suits and sporting identical haircuts. Their facial hair is trimmed to match. So who does she go to?

Finally, one of them speaks, "Fuck, Becca! You just gave me an instant chub!"

Bingo! I found Max!

Rolling her eyes at Max, Rebecca walks into Aiden's arms and gives him a warm kiss. She glances back, and the strange look Max gives when Aiden lets out a deep chuckle as he spins her around for another kiss is alarming. Though not as shocking as when a pair of arms wrap around her from behind. "Okay, that's enough! You win, Max. Let her go."

Fuck! They just played me!

Stepping back, she looks up into the smiling face of the man she was just lip-locked with and deflates. "Christ! How am I ever going to tell you apart now?" She turns toward Aiden with her cheeks burning as she buries her face in his chest. "When you spoke like Max. I thought..."

Laughing, Aiden runs his hand over her hair, an action

she's become familiar with. Only then do her shoulders relax, knowing she's in the right arms. "Oh, it's okay, baby. Max just wanted to test it out."

"Thanks for the kiss, princess," Max says, casually strolling by with a grin. "That was hot. I may have to have more of that later." He slaps Aiden on the back. "All right, let's go for dinner. I'm starved. What's this swanky place called again?"

"It's The Papaya, and it has a 5-star rating in the fine dining section of the resort brochure. Their menu looks fantastic." Aiden hands Rebecca his phone with the menu open. "Here, have a look."

Taking his phone, she scans the menu, ignoring Max's comment about having more of that kiss later. "Mmm, it does look good." Handing Aiden's phone back, she slips her arm through his, continuing in the direction of the restaurant. "So, we just choose a menu plan then, and the courses keep coming?"

"Exactly. In fact, I already chose one for us when I booked our seats. We'll be having the calamari, grilled shrimp skewer and caesar salad starters. Our main course will be the steam lobster with grilled asparagus and rice pilaf." Aiden glances down at her as if seeking her approval.

Smiling, she nods. "That sounds amazing. I'm actually kind of hungry myself."

When they reach the restaurant, the hostess approaches, and Aiden steps forward. "Collins party, please."

Nodding with a pleasant smile, she motions them forward. The restaurant is upscale, with plush seating and fish tanks used as dividers between dining areas. The tables are set with fresh white linen and more spoons and forks than necessary, at least as far as Rebecca and Max are concerned. The hostess leads them to a table in the far corner of the restaurant set for three, with an ice bucket beside the table already chilling a bottle of wine. Aiden pulls out the centre chair for Rebecca and tucks her in, taking his seat next to her.

Once everyone is seated, Aiden pulls the cork on a white citrus flavoured Chardonnay and pours each of them a glass. Within minutes the appetizers start coming.

The calamari is so tender they melt in your mouth, their batter providing just a hint of lemon as it hits your tongue. Rebecca could devour them all night, but they're quickly replaced with garlic shrimp skewers followed by small bowls of caesar salad. In fact, she's almost full when the main entree finally arrives. A large plate with a freshly steamed lobster, grilled asparagus and rice pilaf is set down in front of her, and she leans back with wide eyes. "Oh my goodness, Aiden. Where do you expect me to put all this?"

Laughing, Aiden points at Max with his fork. "I had to be sure the growing boy had a full stomach before we head out for the evening."

Suddenly, Rebecca remembers the cover band at the central pavilion tonight. "Oh no, I hope we didn't miss the show!"

Max rolls his eyes, cracking into his lobster claw. "You know we're at a Jamaican resort, right? We must have heard One Love at least ten times since we've been here already. We're never too late to hear Bob Marley, and I'm sure if you request anything by Marvin Gaye, they'll play it. Now, just relax and enjoy your meal."

Completely gorged, they leave the restaurant much slower than they had arrived. Aiden slings his arm over Rebecca's shoulder and kisses the top of her head. "Well, shall we see if we can still catch that cover band?"

Nodding excitedly, she looks up and grips his jacket. "I'd really like to."

Sliding up beside them, Max pats Aiden on the shoulder. "Sure, let's go see if they can sing like the real M & M's," he laughs. "Get it? Marvin and Marley – M & M's." Rolling their eyes, they shake their heads. "Pfft, whatever. That was funny," Max says, walking ahead.

Aiden takes Rebecca's hand. "What do you say we go back and get changed into something a little more comfortable before we head over to the dance hall?"

"I'm all for that," Rebecca sighs, rubbing her stomach.

She slips on a pair of Lycra shorts and a tank top while the guys put on a pair of black shorts and a white t-shirt, keeping up with their twin style for the night.

Unfortunately, when they reach the central pavilion, the cover band has already turned the show over to the DJ. Still, they decide to stay. Max spots a free table beside the dance floor and waves them toward it. "Let's grab a table, and I'll order us some drinks." Aiden pulls out Rebecca's chair while Max orders. "A round of vodka shooters and beer chasers, please."

When the shots arrive, Max swirls his hand around the

table, asking for another round, and Aiden raises his glass with a simple statement. "To us."

As the waiter brings the second round, Max raises his brow at Aiden and lifts his glass. "I think what you meant to say, bro, is this," – he puts his hand over his mouth and clears his throat, then locks his eyes with Rebecca's – "Ahem. To the three of us. May our days be filled with fun, our nights full of excitement and our time together last a lifetime." He clinks his glass with theirs and slams back his drink.

"Aw, Max," Aiden sniffs. "So sentimental," he winks.

Raising his brow, Max chucks his chin. "That was real shit, and a million times better than" – he raises his glass and twists his lips – "to us."

"Yeah yeah."

"You two seem different since the spa. What have I missed," Rebecca asks, swinging an accusatory finger between them.

Passing a look between themselves, the corners of their mouths tug downward as they shrug. Aiden reaches for her hand. "I don't think you've missed anything, baby. We've just agreed that we're here to enjoy ourselves. So, for the remainder of our trip, we've decided there's no holds barred."

Max smiles slyly at Rebecca and slaps his hand off his knee. "Yeah, what do you say we test that idea. You in, princess?"

Rebecca's brows draw together as she watches Max wave the waiter over and order three lemon drops. "What's a lemon drop," she asks.

Aiden peers over at Max and shakes his head, his gaze turning to Rebecca with a smile. "I'm honestly surprised to hear you ask. It's a shooter. Very similar to a tequila shot. The difference is that this with vodka, lemon, and sugar. Max just likes to get up close and personal when he does them," Aiden says, rolling his eyes.

The shots are delivered to the table along with a plate of lemon wedges and a dish of sugar. Standing beside Rebecca, Max looks down at her and smiles. "Okay, princess. Lick your lips." Grabbing a pinch of sugar, he dabs it along her moistened lips. "Now, let me demonstrate how this is done." Holding the lemon wedge to her mouth, he presses it against her bottom lip. "Here, hold this loosely between your teeth."

Her brow shoots up as she glances over at Aiden. Smiling, he nods. "It's okay, baby, I've seen this before."

She lets Max place the lemon wedge between her teeth and stares up at him as he straddles her lap. "Now, this happens pretty quickly. Are you ready?"

Trying not to giggle, Rebecca repositions the lemon wedge and nods. Max quickly bites into it, removing it from between her teeth, tips back the shot of vodka, then leans down and gently grabs the nape of her neck. His lips cover hers as the sting of vodka passes her sugared lips and fills her mouth. She swallows, his tongue sweeping across hers with a hint of sweetened lemon.

Rebecca's not quite sure what to think as her mind gaps. He looks like Aiden, but his kiss is more intense – much more demanding. Her eyes focus on him as he sits back, sucking the lemon wedge from his lips with a sexy satisfied grin. "Damn, princess. Your mouth is so sweet there's no need for sugar."

She peers over at Aiden, waiting for him to explode, but he doesn't. Instead, he stands and motions for Max to move, taking his place on her lap. Rebecca sits speechless, watching as he dabs some sugar on her already moistened lips, coaxing them open to place a lemon wedge. Aiden shoots back the vodka and lowers his mouth to hers. As he dislodges the wedge, his tongue sweeps across hers.

Jesus, I wonder what these two do with tequila.

He pulls back with a wink leaving Rebecca to lick the remaining sugar from her lips. "Mmm, you're right, Max. There's definitely no need for sugar."

As Aiden lifts himself from her lap, Max takes her hand. "Come here, princess. It's your turn. You think you can manage?"

Rebecca glances at Aiden. "Uh, I'm not sure Aiden would —"

"You're fine, baby. I mean, as long as you're okay with it. It's really just a glorified shooter." He dips a lemon wedge into the dish of sugar and hands it to Max. "Here, we'll make it easier on her."

Max holds up the sugared lemon wedge. "You good, princess?"

She takes a deep breath and nods. "Yep. I guess I'm good."

Aiden hands her the shot of vodka as Max places the wedge between his lips. Holding up the glass, she breathes in through her nose. "All right, here goes nothing." Closing her eyes, she tips it back, then leans forward for the lemon as Max tucks it into his cheek, sticking his tongue out in its place. Rebecca sucks it into her mouth, desperate for the sweetened lemon, when Max grips her bottom, pulling her closer. Consumed by the heat of the moment, she kisses him shamelessly until the tip of her tongue touches the lemon. Then, she pulls back, breathlessly wiping her thumb over her bottom lip, and seeks out Aiden behind her. *Oh my god, what have I done?*

When their eyes meet, she's shocked at his response. Smiling, he holds his hand out. "Now, that was fucking hot, baby."

Rebecca freezes, for a moment wondering if she's made another error in which brother she's staring at. She takes his hand, letting him pull her onto his lap and rest her hand on his swollen groin. "Do you have any idea what that did to me?"

Shaking her head, she stares at him, baffled by his reaction. "I don't understand. You enjoyed watching me make out with your brother?"

Aiden's eyes flit to Max as he shrugs. "I told you this was something we've practiced in the past, Rebecca." Brushing a stray strand of hair from her face, he peers into her eyes. "Max was right. I've been selfish, and I'm sorry. I should never have initiated a contract between us at all, but quite frankly, I didn't know how else to approach you. Max and I had an original plan to share a woman, but I wasn't sure if you—" he stammers, "if I could introduce you to such a thing. You're different. I truly believe you're the one." He takes a breath, collecting himself and smiles.

Rebecca goes to speak, but he raises his hand to stop her. "Please, just let me finish. I've destroyed our contract and had Natasha transfer the remaining $150,000 into your account. So a contract no longer exists between us. Still, I want you to know I'm not opposed to continuing what we've begun" – he gestures between himself and her – "I mean just you and me." His lips tighten into a smile as he takes her hand. "On the other hand, Max and I have a second offer," he says, allowing his smile to broaden. "I'm sure you're aware of Max's feelings toward you. He has made them very apparent, and in case I haven't, you should know that I have completely fallen for you, Rebecca." He glances over at Max. "I guess what I'm trying to say is we'd like you to be ours. Is that about right, Max?"

With his shit-eating grin in place, Max nods. "One hundred percent."

Aiden looks down at her hand as he toys with her fingers. "Worst case scenario for Max and I, you'll decide to leave us behind and reclaim your single status."

Feeling an instant void, she shakes her head. "I don't want to be single again."

Aiden smiles. "I can't tell you how happy I am to hear that, Rebecca, because whatever we have, whatever this is" – he looks at Max and shakes his head – "I'd love to see it develop."

Nodding, she smiles. "I'd like that too."

The song Mine by Bazzi echoes through the speakers, and Max takes Rebecca's hand from Aiden. "Sorry, bro, but things are getting too heavy now, and I think this is my dance."

Leading her onto the dance floor, Max lifts his hand as she holds his finger and spins. When he pulls her back into his chest and snugs up to her backside, her eyes jump to Aiden.

Unaffected, Max places his lips next to her ear, singing the lyrics as his hands trail down the sides of her body and easily recaptures her attention. He lifts her arms behind his head, his hands gliding down the front of her chest to her hips.
"You so fuckin' precious when you smile"
He tugs her back and smacks the cheek of her bottom.
"Hit it from the back and drive you wild"
Spinning her to face him, he grabs her ass, rolling his hips.
"Girl, I lose myself up in those eye-eye-eye-eyes"
Running his hands up her sides, he pushes her arms back up around his neck and kisses her.
"I just had to let you know you're mine –"
Winking, he spins her back around.

When she spots Aiden, he looks focused on their every move. Smiling slightly, he scans the length of their bodies, settling his gaze on the sway of their hips. Max doesn't seem the slightest bit bothered by Aiden's presence as he continues touching her as if he owns her. He repeats his motions, his lips nestling against her ear as he continues to sing.

His hands slowly caressing her breasts before sliding down to her hips.
"Hands on your body, I don't wanna waste no time"
He licks the side of her neck, dropping his hands as he grasps the sides of her thighs.

"Feels like forever even if forever's tonight"
His fingertips slowly drag up her thighs to her hips, and he holds her tight against him,
"Just lay with me, waste this night away with me"
slowly grinding his swelling groin into her bottom.
"You're mine, I can't look away, I just gotta say"
With his arm around her waist, he presses his other hand between her shoulder blades.
"I'm so fucking happy you're alive
Bending her forward, he rolls his hips into her backside.
Swear to God, I'm down if you're down all you gotta say is right"
He spins her back to face him, his mouth falling to hers as he grips her bottom. The press of his arousal against her stomach making her throb.

As the song ends, Rebecca feels another hard body press against her backside and Aiden's deep voice rumbling next to her ear. "Jesus, baby! I wish you could have witnessed how fucking hot that looked." He brushes the hair from her neck and places a light kiss next to her shoulder. "Max is going to add bubbles to his hot tub. You know, have a few drinks. We'd like you to join us. Are you okay with that?"

Nodding, she looks up at Max's smiling face as he takes her hand. "Let's leave your inhibitions here tonight, okay, princess."

Chapter 10 – A Quick Turn of Events

On the way to Max's room, Rebecca stops. "Wait. I should grab my swimsuit."

Aiden takes her hand with a reassuring smile. "You're not going to need that, baby. It's just the three of us. Besides, there's going to be bubbles," he says, gently coaxing her forward toward Max's suite.

Letting them in, Max turns on some music and heads upstairs to his room. He adds some bubbles to the hot tub, mixes a pitcher of vodka and orange juice, then calls them to join him.

When they enter his room, Rebecca points to the tub. "Aren't you gonna get in shit for putting bubbles in there?"

"I'm not worried," Max grins, grabbing the three shots of whiskey he just poured. He holds his arms out, gesturing to the room as he walks toward them. "Why do you think this baby costs so damn much? They expect this kind of shit. Here" – he holds the shot glasses out – "I thought we'd have a shot before we get in the tub."

Taking her shot from Max's hand, Rebecca tips it back and

cringes. "Oh my god! What the hell was that?"

"That, my dear, was a snakebite," Max laughs, taking her glass. "It's a potent little bugger."

"Pfft. You think?"

Chuckling, Aiden runs his hand down her arm and teasingly nips at her bottom lip. "You okay?"

"Yeah, I'm fine. It only burned for a minute. Now I just feel kind of numb," she giggles, stepping closer for a better kiss.

"Mmm, a little numbness isn't all bad." He drops his hands to the hem of her tank top, lifting it over her head as Max slinks up behind her. She stiffens, and Aiden's hand falls to her cheek. "You can tell us to stop at any time."

Her eyes flit to the side – to the gentle kisses moving from her shoulder to her neck. Then, slowly letting them close, she leans into Aiden's lips. The feel of Max growing against her bottom with each light kiss rouses a nervous excitement in her stomach, one she's not sure she should admit. As he reaches around and unclasps her bra, Aiden deepens their kiss.

While her thoughts are lost to soft lips, thumbs hook the sides of her shorts, sliding them down her thighs. Then leaving her naked between them, Max slowly backs away. He pulls off his shorts and turns toward the hot tub. "You guys coming or what?" Climbing in, he lets out an exaggerated breath. "Oh yeah, this feels amazing! What are you waiting for, princess?" He holds up a handful of foam. "We got bubbles," he winks.

Is that it?
Why did I feel like there would be more?
She takes a deep breath.
Because there's always more, Rebecca. You're naked and about to climb into a hot tub with two men – what the hell are you thinking? Of course, there's more you twit!
Her cheeks burning from his stare, she steps into the hot tub and quickly takes her seat, swiping a handful of bubbles onto her chest.

"Nice, right?" Max asks rhetorically with a grin.

Avoiding his gaze, Rebecca nods, her eyes focusing on Aiden as he steps out of his shorts to climb in beside her. He pulls her onto his lap, having to quickly grasp her by the waist to stop her from sliding off. "Shit, Max. What the hell did you use in here? It's like we're sitting in a tub of baby oil."

Laughing, he slips, trying to make his way over to them. "It's just a regular bubble bath, but you're right. It's pretty slick." Holding his hand out to Rebecca, he says, "Why don't you come sit with me, princess. I promise I won't let you fall."

She glances at Aiden as he gives her a nudge and chucks his chin. "Go ahead. I'll get our drinks and grab us each another shot."

Rebecca's flesh ignites as she recalls the feel of Max pressed against her, the warmth of his tongue on her neck. Her stomach twists as she moves toward him.

"There you go, bro. It's good to see you've loosened up," he says, drawing Rebecca into his lap. She loves how her body melds to his – the feeling of flesh against flesh. Max cradles her between his arms, his hands smoothing up her thighs. Then as she slowly starts to slide down his body, he effortlessly slips a finger inside. She lets out a moan, her shameless body pressing into his touch. "That's right, princess, we want you to enjoy yourself. It feels good, doesn't it?"

"Mmhmm." Rolling her head toward Aiden, she can see him watching them. His pupils fixated as he stands with three shots in his hands.

"Okay, take a breather and let's have a toast." Kissing Rebecca, he hands them each a shot. "To us, and a night we'll never forget. May the memories last forever."

Max raises his drink. "Here here!"

Setting their glasses down, Aiden climbs back in and cups Rebecca's face in his hands. His tongue tangling with hers, kissing her as though it will be their last as he pulls her toward him. She falls forward, her hands gripping the seat at his thighs. "Mmm, god damn," Max moans, wiping bubbles from her backside. "Now, that is a sight for sore eyes." Sliding from his seat, he drops his knees between her feet, edging himself forward until his member is pressed against her opening. Rebecca glances over her shoulder, her lids heavy as she licks her lips.

Fuck yeah. I'd have to say that's an okay to proceed.
Max grasps her hips, and she arches her back as he slides inside. Her mouth leaving Aiden's as an airy *'ah'* surrounds them. "Thata girl, princess," Max says, pressing his thumb against her rear entrance as he watches his manhood disappear below.

Rebecca's hand flies to her bottom, glancing back at him with a groan. Max eases up on his thumb as his gentle words of reassurance reach her ears. "Becca, this is meant to be enjoyable, and I promise it will be if you relax your muscles."

"Hey," Aiden places his finger against her chin. "Just concentrate on me, baby."

She nods, but concentration is hard to come by as distractions repeatedly displace her mind. Like the pressure of Max's thumb steadily increasing in her behind. Finally, Aiden reaches below, and she lets out a moan. "That's it, Rebecca, just relax."

Taking a deep breath, she closes her eyes, and Max leisurely replaces his thumb and pushes himself inside. Her moan is long and deep, just like his move. She's not sure what she ever worried about. It actually feels really good.

He pumps a few times, then slowly backs away. Her head flips around when Max reaches for her with a grin. "Surely you didn't think that was it, did you," he asks, hauling her onto his lap and guiding her down on his shaft. "That was only half." He pulls her against his chest and motions for Aiden to move up behind.

Aiden's hand comes to rest on her lower back, and he settles up against her. "Don't worry, baby. I'll go slow," he says, gently pressing into her.

Rebecca's face tightens, and Max quickly captures her lips. His kiss is so demanding that she barely notices Aiden's initial penetration until he's fully seated against her rear. Then her hand flies back, grabbing his thigh, and she cranks her head over her shoulder. "Fuck!"

Aiden pulls back, his face almost as pained as Rebecca's. "Shit, baby. I'm sorry. I should have stopped when I felt you tighten. It's just so god damn good."

She turns back to face Max as he twirls her nipple between his thumb and forefinger. Again, that crazy nervous excitement begins to lurk, but now Aiden has become timid. His movements are so slight that they're nothing more than distracting. He's barely moving as he pulls out slightly, then slowly nudges back in.

Putting her hand on Aiden's thigh to hold him still, she closes her eyes, takes a deep breath and backs herself onto him with a moan. Aiden's eyes open wide as he holds his hands out and watches himself disappear. "Holy fuck, baby! That was perfect."

As he eases out, Max grabs her ass and pushes in, creating a rhythm of alternating thrusts.

Oh – my – god. I've never experienced anything like this before.

Rebecca knows she's moaning, everyone can hear it, but she can't stop – she's lost control.

I may face embarrassment when we're done, but right now, this is fucking heaven.

With each stroke, waves of exhilarating excitement make her body tremble, and she can barely catch her breath. "Holy – shit! I'm gonna cum."

As her muscles squeeze, contracting around them, a chain reaction begins. Max's head falls back with a thundering 'Ahhh' as Aiden thrusts forward with a throaty groan.

Finally, with Aiden draped over her back and her head against Max's chest, she can feel the steady thump of their hearts – it's a melody she won't soon forget. She lifts her head and opens her eyes to Max's blues staring down at her. He kisses her forehead. "Hey, princess, how'd we do?"

Smiling, Rebecca closes her eyes and lets out an embarrassed chuckle. It's that after sex, *'Oh my god, what did I just do?'* kind of embarrassment, and she's not sure how to answer that question without sounding like a complete nymphomaniac.

Geez, Max, you guys did great! When can we do it again?

Aiden slides over beside them, tilting his head to see her face. "Are you okay, Rebecca? I mean, I know you're physically okay, but how are you with what just happened?"

She can feel her cheeks burn as she nods. "I'll admit, I was worried at first, but I actually liked it. I mean, it's not something I'd want to do all the time, but I'd be open to doing it again."

"I'm pretty sure that can be arranged," Max says, kissing her cheek.

Rebecca swats his chest as Aiden pulls her into his lap with a smile. "I'm happy to hear that." He glances over at Max. "And you're absolutely right. This isn't meant to be an all-the-time thing, but it does make for a nice adventure." Kissing her temple, he nudges her off his lap. "Now, I think we could use some one-on-one time. Are you ready to head back to our own room?"

Nodding, she tries to steady herself when Max grabs her arm and pulls her into his lap.

"Goodnight, princess. Thanks for an amazing evening."

"Goodnight, Max. The pleasure was mutual." Taking her hand, Aiden helps her up the steps. She grabs one of the men's dress shirts from the back of the door and holds her finger up. "I've gotta pee before we go."

Smirking, Aiden perches himself by the bathroom door. "Go ahead. I'll wait here."

When Rebecca emerges, he's leaning against the wall waiting patiently. She looks around. "Where's Max?"

Taking her hand, Aiden leads her toward the door. "Oh, he's in the other bathroom, but he said to tell you he'd see you tomorrow. Are you ready to go?"

"Mmhmm."

She no sooner closes the door behind them when Aiden throws her over his shoulder with a roar. "Woohoo! Let's get you to our room so I can ravage you, little missy."

He strides down the path to their suite with Rebecca dangling down his back in a fit of giggles. Kicking the door open, he jogs down the hall to their room and flops her on the bed. Then, jumping over to straddle her, he holds her hands above her head. "I thought I'd never get you all to myself again."

Holding her wrists in one hand, Aiden slowly undoes the buttons on her shirt. "I thought maybe we could use tonight to discover each other. You know, close in some gaps. I want to know more about you." He waggles his brows and drops his eyes to her chest. "I mean, unless you truly are open for more sex. I'm good with that too."

She looks down at her chest as he continues to undo the buttons and raises her brows. "If we're just talking, why are you taking off my shirt?"

He kisses the tip of her nose and opens the shirt, running his hand between her breasts. "Because people tend to bare their souls when their bodies are bare." He stands to discard his shorts then points to the shirt. "Well, let's go, toss it to the floor."

Rebecca sits forward, sliding the shirt from her shoulders and drops it to the floor. "What is it that you want to know exactly?"

Grabbing a couple of beers from the mini-fridge at the end of the room, he cracks one open. "I want to know everything. In return, I'll tell *you* whatever you want." He gives her a kiss and hands her a beer. "There are no wrong answers, Becca. We're just talking life."

Pursing her lips, she nods. "Okay. Max said before that your parents were dead to you both. Why is that?"

Aiden's eyes grow wide. He takes a big slug of his beer and wipes the corner of his mouth with his thumb. "Whoa! Talk about a gutshot right off the bat, Becca." Chuckling, he reaches out and pats her thigh. "Nah, I'm just fucking with you." He rubs his hand over his beard, focusing on something off in the distance and takes a deep breath. "Well, they were never really parents. They'd come by Nan and Pop's maybe once or twice a week at first. Said they had to work a lot, but they weren't working," he says, shaking his head. "They were too busy getting high and gambling." He blows out a breath through closed lips and glances over with a shrug. "Anyway, after a while, they just stopped coming altogether. So, as far as Max and I are concerned – they're dead. It's easier that way." Slugging back his beer, he looks at her and scrunches his nose. "Nan & Pop are our parents – they raised us." He slaps her knee. "Hey! We'll have to take you to meet them. They'll love you." He reaches out and shakes her foot playfully with a smile. "So, what about you? Your parents, your family? You must have someone besides Emma."

Her lips twist as she nods. "Yeah, I have my Dad. I rarely get to speak with him though. He works crazy long hours on the oil rigs in Alberta." She takes a deep breath and thinks for a minute. "I think the last time I actually saw him was three years ago, for about two days. We talk when we can, but it's usually pretty brief." Her frown turns into a big smile as she slaps the bed. "Tell me about your millions. How did you two become rich? I mean, obviously, it's not from an inheritance. Did you win it," she asks excitedly.

Aiden chuckles. "No. We certainly did not win it," he says, peering at her through his brows. "Would you like the short and to the point answer, something in between or the complete painstaking detailed rundown?"

Smiling with her eyes, she thinks about that for a minute. "Oh, I'll take something in between. I mean, unless it's *really* juicy, then I want to hear *every* little detail."

He shoves her back on the bed and opens her legs. Then, climbs between them and lays his head on her inner thigh to get comfortable. "Well, Nan and Pop didn't have a lot of money, and I knew I'd need a college education to be able to make any real cash. So... When Max and I seen an ad for exotic dancers, we decided to go for it. But, don't get me wrong, we only did it until I had enough to pay for tuition, so it wasn't that big of a deal. Besides, the attention of some beautiful ladies wasn't all that unappealing either."

Rebecca laughs, running her hand through his hair. "I bet it was quite the bonus most nights."

Wiping his hand over his face, he nods. "Ah, yes. The work perks! They were the best part of the job," he chuckles. "We had our share of wild nights. We were young, and we had a lot of fun, that's for sure. Anyway, we had spent a lot of time at the gym, so we had the bods." He looks up at her and winks. "There was no question the ladies really dug our looks. We just needed to learn how to dance. One of our friends knew this guy who was a choreographer who had worked out an amazing routine for us. Everyone loved the fact that we were twins, so we danced together. It drove the ladies wild. So they gave us the gig and tagged us Double Trouble." He smirks, patting her leg. "We made a shitload of cash, and I went to college." He takes a deep breath. "When I finished, I found some investors and opened an extremely successful company." He shrugs. "The one you now know as Collins Enterprises. I gave Max 30% of the company because without his help and investment money, I wouldn't have gone through college."

Still stroking his hair, Rebecca looks down at him. "That's pretty amazing. I love that you two are so close, and now I also understand how you're both such great dancers."

Aiden laughs, sitting up to grab his beer. "Yeah, I still really enjoy dancing, especially with you. It's alluring on an intimate level. You're a perfect fit between us, Becca."

Her eyes scan the length of his body while her fingers flit across his chest. "Mmm, you fit nicely too, Mr. Collins."

Before Rebecca even realizes what has happened, Aiden rolls over and crawls on top of her with a growl. "I'm done talking for tonight. How about you?"

She wraps her arms around him and nips at his bottom lip. "Mmhmm. Sometimes talking can be so overrated."

"Mmhmm, like right now," he chuckles. His hand slides between her thighs, running his fingers through her dampness as he glides down her body. "I've gotta have a taste," he says. Then, clasping the back of her knees, he pushes them to her chest and runs his tongue between her folds, right past the very ass he had been buried in only a couple of hours ago.

Her hand flies to his head. "Jesus, Aiden. That's still pretty sensitive. If you want to do this, let's just do it. I don't need foreplay right now."

A moan rumbles from his chest, and he looks up. "Fuck, you sound so hot when you talk like that." He rests back on his haunches and flips her over, pulling her hips toward him. He rubs the head of his dick through her wetness and pushes forward. "Damn, girl, there's no way I can let you go."

This is so unlike him, but I love it!
Rebecca rocks back against him, meeting each thrust of his hips. "Jesus, Aiden, that's deep." He pulls out and slowly grinds himself back in. Her voice deepens with arousal as her head drops forward. "Oh my god, that feels so damn good."

Circling her hips as she tries to keep his pace, she can feel her inner muscles tighten when Aiden slaps her ass and pulls out. "Oh, no. Not yet, princess."

She peers over her shoulder. "Did you just call me princess?"

He smiles, placing himself at the opening of her ass. "I just wanted to see what you'd say." He grips her hips, slowly pressing forward until her body accepts him. Rebecca's breath catches, and he closes his eyes, trying to remain still. "How are you doing?"

She nods, reaching back to place her hand on his thigh. "I'm adjusting, but I'm okay."

Draping over her, he pushes forward with a growl. His hand wraps around her hip, reaching between her thighs. "You feel so fucking good," he says, slamming into her as he rolls her swollen bud between his fingers.

She lets out a husky moan, suddenly finding pleasure again in each stroke. An exhilarating wave of heat ripples through her body, and a loud *"Oh yes"* blurts from her lips. Her muscles clamp down on his shaft like a pulsating vice, and he's moaning alongside her. A roaring *"Fuck yes"* echoes through the room as he grips her hips for a final thrust.

When he releases her, her body falls beneath him, collapsing to the bed. He slowly sweeps the hair back from her face and chuckles. "You okay? You've had an exhausting night."

She doesn't move. A mere groan escapes her. "Mmhmm. I'm fine."

"How about I get you a cloth," he asks, kissing her shoulder.

"M'kay," she mumbles, unable to muster an actual sentence. At the moment, she has one request – sleep, and it's creeping up on her quicker than it ever has.

Aiden pulls her tight to his chest, wrapping his body around her. "Goodnight, princess."

"G'night."

Early the next morning, they wake to loud banging on their door and Max's voice, "Hey! You two better get up. We need to head home."

Rebecca quickly springs up only to have Aiden pull her back down. "Fuck that. He can go on his own. We're staying."

"Aiden, you don't even know what it's about. It must be important. At least go see what's going on." She pulls out of his arms, shrugging on her robe as she makes her way to the door. As she turns the deadbolt, Max is already pushing through. "Sorry, baby." He stabs his hand through his hair. "Where is he," he asks, walking straight toward their room.

Noticing he's on a mission, she follows along behind him. "What happened, Max?"

"Alex," he says, turning into their room.

"Alex? You mean Alex Healey, my ex," she asks, sitting

down on the edge of the bed.

"What about the little weasel," Aiden asks, propping himself up on his elbow.

"Well, Natasha called. She said Alex Healey called her in a rage. He wants to speak with you." His eyes dart to Aiden behind her. "He claims he has a copy of the contract between Rebecca and me —" He closes his eyes and gives his head a slight shake. "I mean you."

Okay, wait a minute...
She starts taking inventory of the things she should have picked up on but completely missed last night.
Aiden's response when they left Max's room—
Grabbing beer instead of wine—
His kiss—
Calling me princess—
And now this. A contract between Rebecca and me — Fuck!!!
They did it again!!

Rebecca stands, peering down at Aiden lying on the bed propped up on his elbow, her eyes narrowing as they dart to Max. Her hands fly to her hips. "You two are fucking ridiculous!"

The suspected Aiden sits up, looking at Rebecca with his brow raised in question as Max steps forward and takes her hand. "I'm serious, Rebecca. Alex wants to see you by tomorrow at noon, or he's turning the contract over to the press."

Pulling her hand back, she reaches for a pillow from the loveseat behind her and swats him. "Alex? What about you two assholes? You two swapped places with each other last night!" She shoves past the real Aiden, slamming the bathroom door behind her.

Max breaks into laughter as Aiden bangs on the door. "Come on, Rebecca. Let me in. Now is not the time for you to be angry. We swear we won't do it again without your knowledge, but right now, we need to discuss this thing about Alex."

Turning on the shower, she calls out, "You know what? Just book me on a flight back this afternoon. I'll go deal with Alex myself. The contract he has isn't signed by me. I only signed it on your phone. So he's lying."

"Is that true, bro?"

Aiden nods. "Yeah, she never did sign a hardcopy, but she did have a copy of the contract with her." He runs his hand through his hair. "I can only assume he has found the unsigned copy."

Max nods. "Then she's right, bro. Have our lawyers say it's something he made up as a disgruntled ex-boyfriend. They've fended off the press before with false claims."

Aiden takes a deep breath. "Typically, I wouldn't worry. They could sweep this under as a false claim, except *my* signature is on it, along with my cell number. Oh, and did I mention Natasha said he's also threatening to press charges on you for assault and battery? He apparently has witnesses of you smashing his head into my car." He shakes his head. "I'm guessing his witnesses are little miss Emma and possibly some of his band members. Anyway, Natasha's calling our lawyers, but we still need to get back. Rebecca shouldn't have to deal with this dick on her own."

As Max stabs his legs into a pair of track pants, his eyes

dart to Aiden. "Oh, she won't. We'll go."

Walking out of the bathroom with a towel around her head, she fixes her gaze on them and purses her lips. "I truly am sorry about the trouble Alex is causing. I'm not sure why he's being such an ass, but—" She waves her finger between Aiden and Max with a perturbed gaze. "Just because I feel responsible for the trouble, don't think I forgot about you two swapping places. I'm still mad about that."

Swatting her bottom, Max leans down and kisses her cheek. "Yeah, but you have to admit, last night was pretty fucking amazing, Becca."

A small smile tugs at her lips. "That doesn't make it okay."

"No, it doesn't." Wrapping his arms around her, Aiden kisses her forehead, then leans back with a smile. "You're right, we were wrong, and we're sorry. Aren't we, Max?"

Smiling, Max shrugs, giving her a wink. "I'm not sorry for spending the night with you, Becca, but I am sorry we lied."

Aiden shakes his head. "Anyway, as for this Alex thing, this isn't on you. We'll fix it together. Don't worry."

"Actually, it is on me. I left the contract in my desk at home. I knew he'd be there with Emma. I should never have trusted either of them. This is my fault."

Max cups her chin, lifting her head to face him. "Becca, this guy and your sleazy friend had no business going through your room. This isn't your fault. Aiden's right. We'll go back and deal with this together." He starts to walk away, then turns with his hand out. "Oh shit! If you and Aiden get married here first, then that contract is truly nothing more than an engagement arrangement – a prenup." He jumps on the bed with a grin. "Fuck, I should have taken law! Get our lawyer on the phone, bro! I bet that'll work!"

Aiden pulls out his phone and dials their lawyer handing the phone to Max. "I hope you know what you're talking about." He peers over at Rebecca. "Are you even willing to marry me?"

Rebecca's stunned. "Uh, you mean like a real marriage?"

Smiling, Aiden throws his arms around her. "Yeah. Like a real marriage. We can get married here this afternoon then fly out this evening. Then, when Alex sees you tomorrow, you'll be Mrs. Aiden Collins, and that contract will mean absolutely nothing," he says, unable to contain his grin.

She stares up at him with wide eyes. "Wow, Aiden. That's a bit drastic. Don't you think? Can't we just go back and let your lawyer handle this? I mean, marriage is forever in my world. I need some time to think about something as serious as marriage." She slowly sinks onto the bed as though her body is a deflating balloon and puts her head in her hands.

Christ, these surprises never stop with these two.
This is it. This must be where I get punked! It took a while, but I knew it was coming.

Max hands Aiden the phone. "Here, bro. You need to send him a copy of the contract, but he says it'll deflect any nonsense Alex may try to cause with the press."

Grabbing the phone from Max, he sends a copy of the contract to their lawyer and within minutes, the phone rings. He answers it, walking out of the room to take the call.

Taking Rebecca's hands, Max peers into her eyes. "Listen, fuck the press. They make shit up all the time. Besides, it'll only be popular until the next big story, that's what, a few days, maybe a week? Trust me, Aiden can handle this, princess." His eyes soften as he stares down at her. "The real question is... do you love him enough to get married today?"

She searches his eyes for the answer, but it's not there. "I- I'm not sure."

Max pulls her into his chest and kisses the top of her head. "It's okay. Don't do anything you're not ready to do. It was just an idea. Maybe a stupid one. I kind of thought you two were already talking about marriage, that's all."

Shaking her head, she smiles, suddenly unsure of herself. "It's just – I don't know what this is between us. I mean, I really love you guys. You two could grow on someone very quickly, and you have." A nervous laugh escapes her as she watches Aiden enter the room with a huge grin. She steps away from Max. "I'll be right back." Gesturing over her shoulder, she smiles. "Bathroom."

Punching in the code on the safe, she snatches out her passport and drops it into her purse, then heads back to hear what Aiden has to say.

"Max, you're fucking brilliant! It'll absolutely work." He stands in front of Rebecca and takes her hands. "Well, what do you say we just do this? Let's turn this adventure into forever." His smile is so bright, his cheeks nearly reach his eyes.

Rebecca looks up at him with a forced smile. Her knees wobbling as she steps back. "I-I'm, uh. Okay, Aiden, let me go grab my things from Max's room and take some time to digest everything."

Max and Aiden give each other a quick glance as Rebecca turns to leave. "Of course, just don't be too long. We need to book the officiant for this afternoon, and I'm sure you'll want a dress," Aiden calls out.

Glancing back, she smiles, giving him a quick nod. "Right. I won't be too long. I just need some processing time." Reaching the door, she stops and turns back to face him. "Aiden, I truly do love you."

Smiling, he blows her a kiss. "I love you too, Rebecca."

Aiden stabs his hand through his hair and looks down at his watch for the 20th time as he paces by the window. "It's been almost two hours, Max. Something isn't right. I'm going to go get her."

Standing abruptly, Max wastes no time following behind him. "Hang on, I'm coming with you. She's in my room after all."

When they arrive at Max's room, it's empty. They call out for her, but there is no sign of her anywhere. Aiden flops down on the sofa running his hands through his hair. "Fuck! She wouldn't have gone back to Victoria alone. Would she?"

Max steps out of his bedroom with a note in his hand and gives it to Aiden. "I'm sorry, bro. It looks like she left."

Looking up at Max, his face drops as he takes the note

from his hands.

Dear Aiden,

I'm sorry. I'm not sure I'm ready to commit to forever yet. I will take care of Alex. You don't have to worry about that. I'll tell the media and anyone else that asks we were dating. Hell, I believed we were anyway. I'll let them know we had a fight here in Jamaica when I told you about a fake contract I had drawn up as a joke.
Please don't misunderstand my leaving. I think you two are great but forever is a really long time. I hope you can find it in your heart to forgive me.

Rebecca xo

Tossing the note to the floor, he glares back up at Max. "God Damn it! Call Andre and get the fucking plane ready!"

Chapter 11 – Oh, Hell No!

Marriage? Oh, hell, no!

Rebecca grabs her passport from the safe and detours to Max's suite. No, she doesn't really need time to make a decision. Her mind is already made up. She has no intention of marrying anyone today. The only thing she'll be doing is grabbing the next flight out of Jamaica.

Wearing only flip-flops, a bikini top and a pair of shorts, she throws on one of Max's shirts and leaves a note for Aiden on the dresser in Max's room. There's no way she's about to be forced into a lifelong commitment over a 30-day contract. When she makes that kind of decision, it will be solely based on love.

The next flight to Victoria has a brief stopover in Toronto, and it doesn't leave for another three hours, but it's her only option. Surely if she waits in Max's room, they'll come looking for her before then. So, she grabs her purse and takes a taxi to the airport.

Her nerves are exploding. Rebecca knows she should have said a proper goodbye to Aiden and Max, but there is no way they would have let her leave without them. If she knows anything about the Collins brothers, they won't be far behind. Her biggest dilemma at this moment is the fact that she's booked on a 10-hour commercial flight home that doesn't leave for another 3 hours. That means there's a possibility that she won't even beat them back.

After witnessing the way Max handled Alex that day at the Purple Lion and now hearing he wants to press charges against Max for trying to protect her, it's best if Rebecca goes alone. Besides, she's already thought about what to say. Sure, it might be a lie, but Alex has lied to her many times. So why would she feel guilty lying to him about something that's none of his damn business?

When Rebecca arrives at the Sangster International Airport, she checks in and passes through security. Then, wanting to be out of direct view should Aiden and Max decide to come looking for her, she makes herself comfortable in a booth near the back in Air Margaritaville.

She's sipping on her margarita when finally, after what feels like an eternity, they call her flight. 'Now boarding flight 1804 to Toronto on Air Canada Rouge. All passengers, please make your way to gate 19.'

With a breath of relief, she grabs her purse and heads for the gate. Handing over her identification, the flight attendant waves her through. It's just over four hours to get into Toronto, but at least there is no juggling of planes. While they sit waiting for new passengers to board, Rebecca takes a minute and checks her phone. The first message is from Aiden.

Rebecca, I'm not angry. Please do not meet up with Alex on your own. Wait for us at my house. The entry code is the day we met 9202017.

The thought of him changing his entry code to the day they met only reinforces the fact that she needs to deal with Alex once and for all. Besides, it's her fault he found that damn contract, to begin with.

She swipes Aiden's message closed and opens the next one from Max.

Princess, text me when you land. We just need to know you're safe. If you are meeting up with Alex, and I have a sick feeling you are. Please promise that you'll stay in a public place.

Rebecca starts to type out a response to Max, letting him know she's okay, then stops and turns off her phone. It's been almost eight hours since she left them in her and Aiden's room. For all she knows, they could be just about to Victoria themselves by now, and there's still another four and a half hour flight ahead of her. If she sends a response to Max now, they'll surely be waiting for her at the airport instead of checking Aiden's and her place first. She needs that extra time to try and convince Alex to give her back the contract.

As expected, she can't seem to sleep a wink on the remaining flight from Toronto to Victoria. Instead, her mind continually slides to thoughts of Aiden and Max. Surely they're back in Victoria by now.

What will she say to Aiden when she sees him again? Is sorry really going to be enough to mend their budding relationship, considering the way she left? Sure, he dissolved their contract, but deep down, she feels as if she owes him something better than disappearing without a goodbye. And Max, he planned the trip to Jamaica to keep Alex away from her and here she is going to meet him.

Her mind has been racing the entire flight, and her body is tight with tension as the pilot activates the seatbelt sign and announces their descent. She's not typically a nail-biter, but her thumbnail has been chewed down so far that she can taste blood.

Maybe she should have just married Aiden. On the one hand, she feels foolish running from the man who has been nothing but kind and understanding. However, on the other hand, if she doesn't deal with Alex on her own, she knows he will continue to make their lives miserable.

When Rebecca's flight lands, she pulls out her phone and calls Alex. Hearing his voice on the other end, she wants so badly to hang up.

'Hello'

"Alex. It's Rebecca."

Strangely enough, the asshole almost sounds shocked to hear from her. As if he wasn't the one who demanded that she come back, or he'd send a copy of that stupid contract to the press.

'Wow! Hey, Becca. Where are you?'

Rolling her eyes at his exaggerated tone, she grabs the strap of her purse and fastens it over her shoulder and heads down the aisle to exit the plane. "Where the hell do you think I am, Alex? I just landed in Victoria. I'm walking off the plane."

Exhaling into the receiver, he pauses.

'Are you alone?'

She doesn't even try to disguise her annoyance as the words rush into the phone. "Christ, Alex! Of course, I'm alone! I believe you have something that belongs to me, and I'm here to get it back. Now, stop with the damn games. I don't have time for this nonsense. I have a life to get back to, and it no longer involves you."

Hearing gravel crunching as he breathes through the phone, Rebecca can picture him jogging down his driveway as he speaks.

'Give me ten minutes, and I'll pick you up in front of arrivals. I'm already in my truck.'

"Fine." Just as she thought, Rebecca hears the truck's engine come to life, but before she can hang up, Alex calls out to her.

'Hey, Becca.'

"What, Alex?"

'I might have made a mistake, but I still love you.'

With little interest in entertaining his remark, Rebecca disconnects the call. Instantly, her phone begins to vibrate, her screen lighting up with missed messages from Aiden and Max.

Aiden—
'Rebecca, we're in Victoria and have been to both my house and yours. Where are you, baby? I swear I'm not upset with you, but I am worried. Please, let me know you're okay.'

A stab of guilt grabs her, and she can feel her heart sink as she reads Aiden's message. She really does owe it to him to let him know she's arrived and is safe. She sends him back a quick text.

"Aiden, I'm fine. Please don't worry. I'll text you soon."

Max—

'Princess, just text me when you land. I promise we're not mad. We just need to know you're safe.'

'Hey, Max. I'm sorry for the way I left, but you did tell me not to do anything I wasn't ready to do. Anyway, I just wanted to let you know I'm back in Victoria, and I'm safe. Alex is on his way to meet me. I'm going to get that contract back. Please don't worry. I'll be sure we stay in a public place.'

As she slips her phone back into her pocket, Alex's big blue 4x4 pulls around the corner, and her heart immediately starts to race. Damn, she can't believe she agreed to meet up with him.

The truck screeches to a halt alongside her, and the driver's door springs open. She freezes when he rushes to her side with a wide smile. His arms wrap around her, and he places a kiss on her forehead. "God, I'm so glad you're back. I've missed you so much."

She briefly recalls when his arms were a comfort, when his kiss made her weak, but those days are long gone. Now his kiss makes her feel queasy, and all she wants is to break free of his arms.

"Alex, stop! This isn't a social call. I came so you wouldn't try to ruin a good man's life over bullshit. That contract was supposed to be a personal joke between Aiden and me. I drew it up on his computer from one of his templates. It was never meant for anyone's eyes but ours." Breaking free of his grasp, she glares up at him. "And you had no business being in my fucking house."

Shocked by her reaction, Alex lowers his eyes to hers with a crooked smile. "You seem to forget that Emma and I are friends. I was invited there."

He reaches for her hand to help her into his truck, but she pulls it away. "Don't touch me. I can get in myself."

Throwing his hands up, Alex steps back with a smirk. "Okay, well, I'm sure you must be hungry after your flight. Is Fish on Fifth still one of your favourites?"

Rebecca is so nervous she ignores his question, settling into the passenger seat as he shuts the door. As she watches him walk around the front of the truck, she takes a deep breath and tries to steady her shaky hands.
God, have I ever felt this nervous around him before?

When he jumps into the truck, he rests his arm over the steering wheel and peers over. "Why are you so damn nervous, Becca?"

"I'm not."

He flicks his finger between them. "This is you and me. It's been us since we were kids. We're just gonna go for dinner and talk. Surely you're not afraid to be alone with me, are you?"

When she doesn't answer, he shakes his head. "Jesus Becca. I haven't been gone that long." He flops back against his seat and starts the engine. "You never did say. Is Fish on Fifth okay?

There is only one thing on my mind, Alex. That's to get the contract back. But I did promise to stay public. Staring out the front window, she nods. "Sure, I guess I could use something to eat."

On their way into Sidney, Alex keeps glancing in her direction. She knows he's dying to spark up a conversation, but she's not about to initiate one. Finally, he can't refrain any longer. "So, how was Jamaica? Did you have a good time?"

God, she wants to smack him in the mouth. He knows damn well she had to cut her vacation short to deal with his childish nonsense. "It was great until we were ignorantly disturbed with false accusations of Aiden making an indecent proposal."

"False accusations?!" Alex's voice is stern as he glances at her with a raised brow. "Come on. Let's not play games, Bec. This is me you're talking to, and don't forget I have a copy of that contract."

"How many times do I have to tell you? It's not a real contract! You have a fucking prank that I typed up for my boyfriend!" She slaps her hands against the seat, wanting desperately to lunge at him. "Look, Alex. The first time Aiden set eyes on that document was when he received the copy you sent Natasha. I hadn't even had a chance to give it to him yet!"

Parking out front of the restaurant, he turns to face her, tipping his head at her in question. "Really, Becca? Is that so? Then tell me something. How did his signature get on the contract, and why is his cell number written on the top?"

Attempting to look calm, she shrugs slightly. "Like I said, it was a template for Natasha, so Aiden doesn't have to be there for every document. I added his cell number to make it look authentic."

"To make it *look* authentic?" He throws his head back with

laughter. "Oh, now that's a good one."

Rebecca's eyes narrow as she tilts her head. "How did you know it was Aiden's cell number written on the top?"

Pulling his keys from the ignition, he shrugs. "How else? I phoned it." Jumping out of the truck, he meets her at her door just as her feet hit the sidewalk. "I would have helped you down."

"Thanks, but I don't need your help," she says, ducking under his arm and striding toward the restaurant.

He stands back, shaking his head as he watches her yank the door open with a huff. "Wow. I'm not sure I've ever seen you act like this much of a bitch before, Becca."

She shrugs. "Well, if you give me back the damn document, you won't need to see any side of me again, Alex. That's the only reason I just spent 10-hours on a flight back here. It certainly wasn't to sit and chit chat with you." She sits at a table against the window and stares at an older woman reading at the bus stop to avoid eye contact with him. "I mean, at this point, I'm considering having you charged with break and enter as well as theft of my personal property."

From the expression on his face, it looks like she's finally gotten his attention until he leans forward and licks his lips. "Come closer. There's something else I need to tell you."

She leans forward, and chills travel down her spine as his lips brush against her ear. "I did take a pair of your panties," he whispers before leaning back with a condescending smile.

His hand snaps up to grab her wrist, mere seconds before she can connect with his face. "Whoa. Relax. Emma invited me over. I didn't break into anything except your laundry hamper." He releases her wrist with a chuckle. "Are you really going to try and have your boyfriend charged with keeping a pair of your panties? Because I'm pretty sure that's not going to stand up in court."

"You're not my fucking boyfriend!"

He shrugs. "You're right! I'm supposed to be your god damn fiancé."

"I am not your fiancé. We haven't been together in over a year, Alex. I have a boyfriend now. His name is Aiden. What I want to know is, if you didn't break into my room, how did you get the document?"

Rolling his eyes, he shakes his head. "Come on, Becca, call it what it is, for Christ's sake. It's a god damn contract between you and Collins for sexual services in exchange for money. It's not a pretend document. And for your information, the contract was sitting on your kitchen counter when I went over to see Emma. She said she found it in your desk drawer when she was searching for a pair of scissors."

Folding her arms across her chest, she feels the heat rush to her face.
Emma needs a damn throat punch. Looking for scissors, my ass – she was snooping.

"So the pair of you are nothing more than snoops, thieves, and liars. You two deserve one another."

Drawing his brows together, he leans forward, slamming

his fist on the table. "I don't want Emma!"

"You wanted her just fine that day I brought my new car by the Purple Lion. You know, the day you had your tongue lodged down her throat," Rebecca shoots back a little harsher than intended.

She smirks, watching him chew on the inside of his cheek.

Ah, apparently, you weren't aware that I knew about that minor incident. Huh, Alex?
Score one for Becca!

Not ready to let it go, she continues. "Oh, yes. I know all about that little indiscretion between you and Emma. Not that it matters now. Emma was only the icing on the cake. I've watched you parade around with several women publicly over the past year, don't forget. I'm numb to it all now." She waves her hand through the air as if brushing it off like yesterday's news. "I knew the moment you left. We were never getting married. It might have hurt for the first few months, but that feeling has long since passed. Now, I feel nothing for you."

Alex reaches for her hand, and for the first time, she can see regret in his eyes. She reminds herself, *'too little, too late'* and pulls her hands back, placing them in her lap. "Don't touch me, Alex. Just don't."

Acknowledging her reaction with a smirk, he waves to the waitress for the check. "Fine. Let's go for a walk. We can talk out on the pier while we get some air. You love it out there, right?"

"I really just want the document back. I think it's evident there's nothing left between us. I mean, Christ, when have you not cheated on me? I'm not a kid anymore, Alex. I need someone I can trust, and clearly, that's not you."

The waitress drops the check on the table and stands with her hand on her hip, staring at Alex. Instantly, Rebecca can feel her cheeks start to burn.
Oh, this is just great! Another one of his trollops, I presume.

He peers up at the waitress with a sour face. "Thanks. I'll bring it up to the register. Now, if you don't mind, we're talking."

The waitress slaps her palms down on the table, bringing herself to eye level, glances at Rebecca, then glares at Alex. "I thought you said you were done with her. Why haven't you returned my calls?"

Rebecca rolls her eyes and shakes her head.
Yep. Seen that coming a mile away.

His eyes narrow than his face drops.
Ahh, shit! Perfect timing. It's that chick from the night before I left town. What's her name again?
Squinting up at her, he snaps his fingers and points. "Bethany, right?"

Her brows shoot up as her mouth twists. The annoyance evident in her tone as she stands, with her hand on her hip. "Pfft! It's Brittany."

"Right. Well, Brittany. As you can see" – he throws his hand out, gesturing to Rebecca – "Things have changed." Then, shrugging, he feigns a smile and turns his attention back to Rebecca.

A very unimpressed Brittany kicks his chair and walks away in a tiff. Rebecca holds her hand out toward the pissed off waitress and raises her brow. "There you go—just another notch on your belt for you. I rest my case, Alex. There's no us."

Exhaling through pursed lips, he tosses a fifty on the table and holds his hand out to her. "Let's take a walk. We need to talk."

Ignoring his outstretched hand, Rebecca gets up and walks toward the door. Once they reach the sidewalk, she swears she catches a glimpse of Max's hummer, but when she looks back, it's gone.

It's getting late, and she's completely done with the pleasantries. If Max and Aiden are in the area, she needs to get that contract and get away from Alex. Scowling, she shifts her weight to one leg. "Come on, Alex. Where's the goddamn contract? I just want it back. We have nothing to talk about."

The corner of his mouth tightens as he nods. "Actually, we do, but if that's what it'll take for you to talk to me. Just give me a minute, and I'll grab it."

Taking off toward the truck, he returns with a manilla folder stuffed under his arm. "Okay? Now can we please go for a walk? You can have it once we get out on the pier." He starts walking, glancing back to wave her forward. "Well, come on."

"Ugh!" She strides up beside him, walking in silence along Bevan Avenue toward the pier. The moment they step onto the first wooden plank, Rebecca holds out her hand. "Okay, we're here. Now, let me see the document."

His eyes open wide, and he hands her the folder. "Wow,

Bec. With that attitude, there's no way it's just a gag. It's a valid contract, just like I said."

Snatching the folder from his hands, she opens it to find it empty. Her face begins to burn as she glares up, slamming the folder against his chest. "Alex, stop screwing around! Where is it?"

"I'm not that stupid," he laughs, grabbing her by the arm. "Once I hand it over, you'll leave, and I'm not done talking yet."

Lowering her voice, she grits her teeth and tries to pull free. "Then say what you have to say. I've had a long flight, and I'm too tired for these games."

"I'm not playing a game with you, Becca. I'm trying to explain. Now, walk with me." He tugs her forward. She follows along, trying to avoid a scene as he talks. "You see, Becca. Men have stronger urges than women, and you never quite understood that, did you? I tried so hard, but you just wouldn't give in, and the chicks – god, the chicks were throwing themselves at me like you can't imagine. What was I supposed to do?"

He glances down at her, but her gaze doesn't waver from the ocean. "Obviously, you haven't been saving yourself for me." He laughs. "I mean, you put on this good girl act, but there's no way that you can tell me you haven't been fucking Collins, can you?" Tugging her back, he stops and peers into her eyes. "Well, can you?"

Trying to free her hand, he squeezes it tighter. "It's none of your damn business who I fuck!"

With a quick snap, he pulls her against his chest and

speaks through clenched teeth. "Now see, Bec, that's where you're mistaken. You are very much my business. In case you've forgotten, we promised each other forever, remember?" Taking her hand, he examines her finger then holds it up to her face. "Why the fuck aren't you wearing my ring?"

"Oh, don't look so surprised. I haven't worn it since you left. You never called except for a handful of times, and you only text me the first month you were gone. You wanna tell me why I would wear your ring?"

Pulling from him, she walks further along the pier, kicking a stray stone off into the water. Finally, she leans against the railing and looks out across the ocean. "I never said I'd wait for you, and you sure the fuck didn't wait for me."

Something in him shifts, and his voice softens as he stands next to her. He fans his hand out toward one of the fishing balconies. "Hey, remember that balcony over there? We used to come out here to make out. In fact, I'll bet our names are still carved in that bench."

Glancing down, he nudges her elbow and points to the small loading dock with a chuckle. "And there — remember when we went skinny dipping that night?" He ducks down to look into her eyes with a cute smile. The same smile she's sure must have broken hundreds of hearts over the past year. "Remember? That's the night you lost your virginity. We were right there under the pier." He nudges her elbow again. "Come on, Becca, doesn't that mean anything to you?"

Shaking her head, she turns to look back out across the

ocean. "No, Alex. It doesn't mean anything to me anymore. Those days are so far removed from my present. In fact, I barely recall any of my time with you. In all honesty, that all feels like it was a lifetime ago."

Stepping up behind her, he grabs hold of the railing, caging her between his arms and presses his groin tight against her bottom. He leans his head against hers, nuzzling his nose into her hair and whispers. "Well then, maybe we just need to make some new memories."

As his lips brush her neck, she jerks her head away. "Christ, Alex. Just stop!"

Exhaling, he rests his chin on her shoulder. "Look, I get it. I screwed up. Just tell me what it will take to bring you back to me."

"I'm not coming back to you. That's not why I'm here."

"I personally never thought you were one for money, but shit, if that's what it takes these days. Then name your price. Tell me, how much will it cost me to steal you back from Collins?"

Rebecca feels the heat flood her body as she tries to spin out from his arms, but Alex grabs hold of her hands. He folds them into a hug across her stomach, pressing his body tight to hers and inhales against her neck. "Mmm. My god, you smell so fucking good."

She tries to pull her arms free, but he tightens his grip, letting out a sinister chuckle next to her ear. "Damn, you've gotten feisty, Bec. I'm not judging you. I'm asking you a serious question. How much will it cost me to get you back? It was $300,000 that did it for Collins, right?" He rubs his erection along her bottom. "I'm good for that, but I want more than 30 days."

"Let me fucking go!" She twists in his arms, trying to break loose. Her voice cracking as she speaks. "No amount of money could ever bring me back to a cheater like you."

"Oh, come on. We aren't kids anymore. I know Collins has money. He bought you an expensive car — he has a big house — takes you on expensive vacations. I get it. I can play that game too. I have money now, so just tell me. What is it that will make you happy again? Will a nice house and a half a million bring you back to me for good?"

He spins her around to face him, keeping a firm grip on her hands. "What the fuck is wrong with you? This isn't about money," she spits. "The problem is you. You can't keep your dick in your pants!"

As he glances down to size up his crotch with a cocky smirk, she brings her knee up, connecting a solid crack to his groin and sends him to his knees. "What the fuck, Becca?! Why do you always have to be such a fucking bitch?!"

Finally free of his grasp, Rebecca darts for the walkway at the end of the pier. "Fuck you, Alex!"

As she shouts back over her shoulder, she collides full force with a solid body. Two big arms wrap around her, and that familiar intoxicating smell of citrus spice wafts a sense of security straight to her nose. She gasps, trying to catch her breath as she lifts her head to see Aiden's welcoming eyes.

Gently brushing the hair from her damp face, he smiles.

"You're okay, baby. I got you."

"Oh, Aiden, I'm so sorry." Tears flow freely down her cheeks as she melts against his chest. "I thought I could get the contract back, but he wouldn't give it to me. I told him I made it up as a gag, but I don't think he believes me."

"Shh, don't worry about it," he says, cupping her face in his hands, his thumbs wiping her tears away. "It's going to be fine. All that matters is that you're okay." He kisses her on the cheek and tucks her into his side. "Let's go home."

Nodding, she turns to look back. "Wait. Is that Max?"

Tucking her back into his side, Aiden continues to walk them off the pier. "Max is fine. He'll meet us at the car."

As they step onto the walkway, Aiden turns her to face him. "You know we have no contract between us any longer, right? So if you wanted to leave, you didn't have to run. There is no penalty or repercussions. You do understand that, don't you?"

She starts to say something, but Aiden places his finger over her lips. "Shh, just let me finish." He leans her against Max's truck and takes her hands. "I didn't come because I thought you were running from me, Rebecca. I came because I think you were trying to protect me from the publicity, and make no mistake. A publicity blooper is never anything I care to experience. Still, it will never rate above your safety." Placing his hand under her chin, he lifts her face. "I'm sure you must know by now that Max and I care about you."

"I don't want people to know how we began, and I'm sure you don't either. It's like our dirty little secret that I'd like to keep buried. I told you from the start I didn't need a contract, but you wanted to be able to walk away after 30 days guilt-free if it wasn't what you wanted. Contract or no contract, I would have at least taken the chance." She fixes her eyes on his. "Believe it or not, I think I actually love you, Aiden."

The muscles in Aiden's jaw tighten as he forces a smile. "Yet, the marriage proposal scared you away."

Chuckling, she shrugs. "It was for all the wrong reasons. Besides, This is still really new. I'm not convinced we're ready for marriage. Are you?"

"I'm a decision-maker, Rebecca. I make my mind up on things very quickly. Some people say, 'if you snooze, you lose.' Well, I have to agree. Marriage has never crossed my mind before, and yet, I would, without question, marry you tomorrow." Kissing her lightly, he looks into her eyes. "I know I love you."

Oh god, please don't propose again.
Trying to steer from the marriage topic, she scrunches up her nose and asks, "So what do we do about the contract? You know Alex will likely take it to the press now."

"I doubt he will, but if he does, I'll say you drew it up on one of my templates for fun." He shrugs. "That's what you already told him, right? They can make of it what they want. The more I think about it, the less I care. The only thing I care about is that you're okay."

Max's dark shadow jogs toward the truck, his big burly voice carrying through the air before he's in full view. "Damn, Princess! We missed you." He holds his arms out to her. "Well, come and give me a hug, damn it. We just flew 9 hours to come and get you."

Laughing, she jumps into his arms. "You couldn't have missed me that much. It hasn't even been a full 24 hrs yet."

Sliding down, she pats his chest and squints up at him. "Now, stop trying to distract me. What did you do to Alex? I saw you heading for him when Aiden pulled me away."

Max shrugs as he opens her door. "I have no idea where he went. He must have left before I got there."

Nodding, she smiles. "Somehow, I doubt that, Maxwell."

"Oh, I see. It's Maxwell now, is it?" He darts for her, but Aiden steps between, halting them.

"Enough!"

Sticking her tongue out at Max, she laughs as she climbs into the passenger seat. "How'd you two know where to find us anyway?"

Aiden leans on her door and raises his brow with a smile. "Because I listen to you. You told me this was your place," he says, using his fingers as quotations. "Where else would he take you?"

Starting the truck, Max glances back at Aiden. "Are we ready to go home?" His gaze rakes across Becca. "We could always go have a couple of drinks at the Purple Lion and get it all out of our systems in one night. Emma should be working tonight, right?"

Aiden shakes his head. "No, I think we've had enough excitement for tonight. Why don't we go soak in the hot tub? We can have a few drinks and relax."

"Yeah, that sounds good too, as long as I can stay the night. Although, we still have two weeks left in Jamaica if you want to head back there."

"You know my house is your house. I'm open to returning to Jamaica tomorrow if Rebecca wants to go." Swinging his gaze back to meet hers, he gives her a sly smile. "However, I must remind you that my house offers clothing-optional accommodations with absolutely no restrictions on a 24/7 basis."

"Then I guess there's no need to go back to Jamaica. I'll admit it was a nice getaway, but it's over now," she says, smiling with a shrug.

Laying his hand over hers, he runs his thumb along the top of her hand. "Maybe we should stop by your place so you can grab some of your things."

She shoots him a worried glance. "Aiden —"

He raises his hand with a slight smile. "I'm not saying we have to get married. I'm simply saying you can stay with me until you decide what you want to do. I know you don't want to go back to your place and I have plenty of room. There'll be no expenses, so you won't have to worry about work for now."

Max glances back at him and smirks. "I'd take him up on his offer, princess. That sounds like a pretty sweet deal. I personally wouldn't go to work for the prick, but as for grabbing your stuff and staying with him, I'd say that's a solid choice. You know Alex will be back at your house to see Emma." He runs his hand across his beard in contemplation. "You can correct me if I'm wrong, but from that knee you delivered to his groin, it kind of looked as if you don't care to deal with him anymore. Am I right?"

Laughing, she slaps the back of his seat. "Wow, you saw that? I never saw you on the pier until after I ran into Aiden."

"Oh, I saw the whole thing. I wouldn't want to meet your knee, that's for sure. You nailed him good."

"I honestly doubt you would ever give me a reason to do something like that to you, Max."

Aiden rubs her shoulder. "So what do you say? Do we go pick up your stuff? It's completely up to you. We don't have to go tonight. We can always go another time. I just thought it may be easier for you since you said Emma's working."

It's not a difficult decision—Aiden's right. With Emma working, the timing is perfect. "Yeah, you're right. Let's go grab it while she's at work. The less I have to deal with them, the better."

"Great! I can stop by my place and grab a trailer," Max says with a wide grin.

"I appreciate that Max, but there's no need for a trailer. I'm not taking any of my furniture, just my clothes and my computer." Feeling his eyes on her, Rebecca looks back at Aiden. "Unless, of course, sharing your bed is no longer an option."

A smile slides across Aiden's face. "I'll expect nothing less."

Max can barely contain his laughter. "Listen to mister prim and proper, *'I'll expect nothing less.'* Come on, Aiden. Just fucking say what you mean." He glances back at Rebecca in his rearview mirror. "Princess, don't let him fool you. What he meant to say is you better have your sweet ass in his bed tonight, or he's hunting you down. Isn't that more like it, bro?"

Aiden draws in a long breath and smiles as he takes Rebecca's hand. "Actually, I thought more along the lines of I can't picture my bed without you in it."

Shuttering with laughter, Max shakes his head and glances back at him. "Yeah. I'll bet that's *exactly* what you meant."

Rebecca throws her arms around Aiden's neck and kisses his cheek. "Aww, baby. I love sleeping next to you too."

When they pull into Rebecca's driveway, she sits forward and points toward the garage. "That's odd. Alex's truck is here." Her eyes dance between Max and the truck nervously. "Of course, I guess if you really didn't see him on the pier. He could have had time to catch up with Emma before she left. I don't see her car."

Putting his truck into park, Max lays his head back against the headrest and looks over at her. "Hey, if you're not comfortable or you'd rather come back another time. That's fine too, but you can be assured that there's no need for you to worry about Alex. We'd never let anything happen to you."

Aiden rests his hand on her shoulder. "Max is right. We'll come in with you to get your stuff."

Resting her hand over his, she smiles. "I know, and really this is still my house, and I'm not the one that's done anything wrong. So, them being here shouldn't stop me from getting my clothing."

"If we're here just for your clothing, I'll take care of anything that needs to be replaced."

"Aiden, you've already bought me a new wardrobe, and I love you for it. I really do." Rebecca frowns as she looks up at him. "That doesn't mean I wouldn't like to have some items that remind me I'm still me."

Slapping his hand off his thigh, Aiden jumps out of the truck and takes her hand to help her down. "Say no more. That I can understand. Let's go get your stuff."

With the guys trailing along behind her, they make their way to the house. Max skips over to Alex's truck and peeks into the window. "Well, he's not in here."

Rebecca opens the front door, and they can hear the thump of bass coming from upstairs. Timidly, she turns around to look at them. "No, but I think he might be inside. Emma wouldn't leave the stereo on and go to work."

Following the music upstairs, they quickly realize it's coming from Rebecca's room. A sick feeling falls in the pit of her stomach as she reaches for the handle and gives the door a shove. Even in the darkness, Emma's squeal cannot be mistaken. Rebecca walks in and flicks on the light.
Jesus Christ! Are you fucking kidding me?

To be continued...

Contracted to Mr. Collins 2

Decisions
Release date July 15, 2021

Did you enjoy the story? Have you considered leaving a review? — There's nothing an author appreciates more than an honest review.

Where to find updates on upcoming books

https://sjturnerstories.com

Twitter or Facebook
https://www.twitter.com/SJTurner_Author

https://www.facebook.com/SJTurnerAuthor

A proud member of the Independent Author Network
https://www.independentauthornetwork.com/sj-turner.html

About The Author

Sj. Turner

SJ. Turner fell in love with literature at an early age. She found herself stealing her mother's romance novels and tucking them under her pillow to read late at night. However, the first novel that truly left an impact was To Kill a Mockingbird by Harper Lee. This story has managed to stick with her throughout the years.

As a teen, she found poetry a valuable source of expressing those deep emotions some teens find challenging to release. So, after several years, she finally submitted a few to a poetry contest. Two of those poems are currently published in a 2002 collection.

By 2018 a family member had suggested writing a book and within a few months, Contracted to Mr. Collins was written. Though it was written mainly to amuse family and friends, the unedited version was uploaded to a self-publishing site. Yes, unedited and open to the public.

Surely you can imagine her surprise to find not only was

it selling but there was a consistent request for a follow-up book as well. Of course, that could only mean one thing. There'd have to be a book 2.

With the readership on the rise, there was only one thing left to do—the Collins books had to be pulled and reworked for a real audience.

Praise For Author

'I'm absolutely in love with this story! SJ. Turner should be named Page Turner. I couldn't put it down. If you loved Fifty Shades, you'll love this book.' — Ella M.

'Loved it! This story is comical, sexual, and captivating! I'm hooked! Great writing style, and the plot is killer.' — Olivia S.

'This author has opened a whole new level of adventure to me. She really had me glued to this book—what an exceptional writer.' — Susan E.

'A page turner. A sensuous, very 50 shades, must read!' — Julie D.

'This is one hot book. Rebecca, Aiden, and Max make a hot threesome. But don't get so involved you miss the other action. I enjoyed it from beginning to end. If you like erotica this is definitely for you.' — Judy F.

'I loved reading this book. The characters hook you, the plot pulls you in, the erotic scenes are hot, and the humour makes it fun.' — Sara P.

'Being an avid reader, I am always looking for topics outside my comfort zone. Romance is generally not my first choice, but after reading the synopsis, I was willing to give it a try. This book delivered to keep me entertained!' — G.B.S

Made in the USA
Middletown, DE
31 July 2021

44570024R00136